MW01479514

Elect

By
Rae Burton

Grandma—

*Happy Birthday!
Thank you for your unwavering support.*

1

Shots fired. Cold steel pressed against her neck. The room spun out of control. Any move could be her last. When would it stop? Her heartbeat exploded in her chest. It was time to end this. Live or die, she didn't care anymore. "Do it now!" She screamed. "Do it now! What are you waiting for?" She cried out.

A shot fired. She felt the breeze of the bullet flying past her cheek. Warm drops splattered on her cheek as she collapsed to the floor. Sweat rolled down her neck. She glanced behind her. His eyes held hers. The hair on her arms stood. His hand rose, aiming the gun behind her.

Her eyes grew large and she reached for the gun. "No!" Her scream echoed along with two gun shots in the empty black room.

"Allie! Allie, wake up!" Strong hands gripped her shoulders, shaking her.

Allie gasped, reaching for the gun under her pillow. It was gone. Her eyes shot open and she stared into Marcus' worried eyes. "Marcus?"

"You're all right. It was just a dream."

Tears welled up in her eyes as she sat up and rubbed her arms. "Will these dreams ever stop?" She shook her head and sighed, swiping the tears from her cheeks.

"The doctor says they should eventually get better." Marcus forced a smile and tucked her hair behind her ear. "We just need to create some happy memories."

"Wow, thanks Dr. Phil." Allie shook her head and swung her feet to the edge of the bed. "They're never going to let me come back to work at this rate. I can't even get a decent night sleep without you here."

"You know I don't mind the couch. It's quite comfortable for a brick-like structure." Marcus put his arm around her shoulders. "And you'll pass that psych eval, shoot the head off some paper target and be back on the streets with me by this afternoon. Third time's the charm."

"Gee, thanks." Allie stood up and went to the bathroom. "I need to move."

"Okay, you up for a run?"

"No, move, like out of this house." Allie wrapped her arms around her middle and surveyed the room. Everything in this room reminded her of

Bastian. He'd been in her house enough that he had been able to duplicate everything about it. She needed to sell this house and everything in it and start over.

"Allie, come on. Where are you going to go? You're still making payments on this house. You're just going to leave it?"

"I'm never going to be able to put this behind me unless I'm out of this house."

"I disagree. You're letting all that psycho-babble get to you." Marcus stood up and went to her bedroom door. "Just give yourself some more time. Things will start looking up, I promise." He tapped her door jamb and left. "I'll get breakfast while you get ready to go. Think positive thoughts!"

Allie rolled her eyes and went into the bathroom. She stared at her reflection in the mirror.

She looked as exhausted as she felt. Her hair was a mess. She'd lost a lot of weight and looked like a wimpy puppy. This was one thing she was never going to get over. Her abduction, Bastian's arrest and Nate's cunning escape would forever be engrained in her mind. She was an utter, miserable failure.

Think positive thoughts. Allie clenched her teeth, turned on the shower and jerked the shower curtain closed. "That's easy for you to say, Marc."

*****

The corners of his mouth turned up in a smile as he watched the family outside. They looked happy, but looks could be deceiving. What looked like a nice family barbeque was most likely an experience they were all pretending to enjoy. No one loved their family that much. They were a bunch of liars.

Tony lit up a cigarette and picked up the file on the seat next to him. He blew smoke from his nose. "Hello, Lancasters." He smiled around the cigarette as he took another puff and flipped to the second page of the report. "Grady and Vanessa Lancaster; married fifteen years, two kids…" He glanced at the house and shook his head. "All this story is missing is the white picket fence."

Tossing the file aside, he opened the glove box and removed a gun and spool of fishing line. The fun was over; it was now time to get to work. He'd let them live three days longer than he should have and he hated to be behind schedule.

He took the cigarette out of his mouth and smoke billowed around him. Smiling, he set the cigarette in the ashtray. He'd be back in a few minutes to finish it. It wouldn't take long to do what he had to do.

Emerging from the car, he tucked the gun and fishing line in his jacket pocket. He zipped his jacket, tugging at the collar. The night had gotten quite chilly. Maybe he should have brought the cigarette with him for the extra warmth.

He trotted up the stairs and rang the doorbell. He cleared his throat and looked up and down the street. Not a soul in sight. The porch light flipped on and he forced a smile when he saw someone peek out the window at him. "Come on Vanessa, open the door. Don't make this difficult." He mumbled through clenched teeth.

The lock sounded on the door and he reached into his pocket for the gun. His smile was genuine when the door opened and revealed his prize.

"Tony, what are you…" She gasped and clutched the door, trying to close it.

He pushed the door open, throwing her back into the entryway table. He aimed the gun at her head. "Hello Vanessa."

*****

Allie's hand slammed down on the stapler, shaking her desk and causing her coffee to spill over on her desk. Marcus calmly picked up the coffee cup and cleaned up the spill. The third time hadn't been the charm. Her psychiatrist refused to release her to active duty. He knew she was taking it hard, but it took every ounce of patience he could muster not to yell at her. The longer Allie listened to that doctor's psych talk, the more she became someone he didn't know anymore.

"That stupid doctor just won't give it up! I don't know what his problem is!" Allie knocked her fist on the stapler again, causing it to jam. She picked up the stapler and pounded it against the desktop. Growling, she threw it down and stood, shoving her chair back. Her finger pointed at his nose. "*You* need to fix this."

"Fix what? If you act like this with him, it's no wonder he won't release you. Just chill."

"I am chill!" She yelled, her finger pointing at the door of her small makeshift office. "The only reason that man won't release me is because he has some silly crush on me."

Marcus scoffed. "I doubt that."

"Why? You don't think it's possible?" She put her hands on her hip and shook her head.

"Contrary to what you might think, not everyone is in love with you, Al." Marcus crossed his arms over his chest. "Maybe he sees this angry side of you and decides it's best not to give you a gun."

Allie narrowed her eyes at him. "Excuse me?"

"Quite frankly, I agree with him." The more they talked, the angrier she got. He'd been joking at first, but the joke wasn't funny anymore. Maybe the doctor and his psycho-babble held some merit.

Her mouth dropped open. "You agree with him?" She exclaimed. "So what? You think I'm some basket case?"

"Allie, that's not it at all. You're just a bit out of control." Marcus nodded toward her chair. "Sit down and just breathe."

Allie slumped down in her chair and pouted.

"And for future reference, you should probably drink decaf." Marcus set her coffee cup down and sat up on her desk. "I'll tell you what, if you promise to drink decaf and work on controlling that temper I find so endearing, I will let you in on one of my cases."

Her head snapped up, hope glittering in her eyes. "You mean it?"

"I mean it. I just got a new case that I can't make heads or tails of but maybe you can find something I missed."

"I usually do." Allie stood up and hurried over to him, resting her hands on his arms. "Do you really mean this, Marc? You may just be saving my life."

Marcus smiled. "Well, it wouldn't be the first time." He winked and stood up, resting his hands on her shoulders. "This is the job you have been given, do your best and I'll bring a case file when I come to your house tonight. Deal?"

"Deal!"

Marcus was glad to see the spark back in her eyes. Maybe what she really needed *was* to get back to work. Maybe the doc and his psycho-babble were wrong. It was hard to tell. He'd reserve judgment for now. "Perfect. Have pizza ready when I get there and we'll make a late night of it. See you tonight." He pressed a kiss to her forehead and left her.

Out in the bullpen, he went to his desk and pulled out the file he'd promised Allie. A family of four had been killed a week ago and he had no fresh leads whatsoever. Allie always helped him get out of his slump, but he had a nagging feeling that maybe this wasn't a good choice. There was a reason the doctor hadn't cleared her yet.

Marcus shook his head and tossed the file on the corner of his desk to take home later. What harm could be done in just showing her a file? It's not like she would be out investigating with him. She'd just be reading some papers. No harm, no foul.

2

The seconds turned into minutes; minutes to hours. She'd been home for four hours and Marcus had yet to come home with the file he promised. The pizza he'd asked for was now cold and hard in the box. She'd attempted to keep it warm the first hour, but had finally given up. Marcus had never lied to her before, but now she was beginning to wonder if a leopard really could change its spots.

Allie sat down on the couch, hugging her knees to her chest. She rested her chin on her knees and looked around the house. The ticking clock echoed around her. Her fingers twitched against her pants. Groaning, she let her feet drop to the floor.

The house was too quiet.

Allie turned on some music and cranked up the volume. Listening to music would calm her and get her mind on other things. Marcus was probably just running late and she had no reason to think he wouldn't be here. He had been here every night, just like he'd promised. He was a good friend, honest. He wouldn't deceive her.

As the music filled the house, her head started bobbing and her feet moved on their own. A smile teased the corners of her mouth as she danced her way to the kitchen to get a drink and some popcorn. She sang at the top of her lungs as she tossed a bag of popcorn in the microwave and pushed the buttons. Pulling out her favorite popcorn bucket, she flipped it up in the air, caught it, and played it during the drum solo of the song.

Tossing the bucket on the counter, she went to get her drink ready. Music never ceased to amaze her. No matter how sad or angry she could get, music would always make her feel better. She bobbed her head back to the microwave and tapped the counter while she watched the popcorn bag spin around.

A chill went down her spine causing the hair on her neck and arms to stand up. Allie stopped all movement and strained her ears. Someone was there and she had no gun. Allie bit her lip and glanced around the kitchen with her eyes, avoiding any movement with her head. Anything could be a weapon. Which weapon should she choose?

Allie crouched down in one swift, easy movement and allowed herself to look around freely. A knife was her best choice but it was too far away. Her next best option was a rolling pin. Her mom bought her a marble rolling pin years ago and that was heavy enough to cause some damage. Allie slipped two drawers over and opened the drawer where her rolling pin was nestled safely inside.

Pulling the weapon from its place, she crept over to the edge of the island, pressing her back against the wood. She glanced around the corner and stared at the window next to her back door. Her music still thundered around her. Any movement she made would be drowned out by the loud guitars. If she was going to make a move, it had to be soon.

A shadow appeared behind the curtain on her kitchen door.

Swallowing hard, Allie moved to the cabinet right next to the door. She gripped her rolling pin, closed her eyes and took several deep breaths. *You can do this Allie. Defend yourself.* The knob turned but the door was locked. There was a tapping around the door, no doubt searching for a key. She didn't have a spare key for the back door so they would either pick the lock or go around to the front. Which would it be?

Allie peered around the corner and stared at the shadow, wishing the person would just go away. If Marcus had been here when he promised, she wouldn't be alone right now. The old Allie would have opened the door and attacked the perpetrator but she didn't trust herself enough to manage such a feat now. Cower and hide was her new motto.

Movement caught her eye and she glanced at the front door. Someone was there. Swallowing hard, she weighed her options. Her head snapped around and she looked back up at the kitchen door.

The shadow was gone. Maybe the person at the front and back was the same person. Either way, she had to move.

Keeping low, she darted to the couch. She crouched behind it, waiting. The front door opened and closed. Allie took a deep breath and counted down from three. When she reached one, she jumped out from behind the couch and toward the intruder. The man caught the rolling pin and jerked it from her hands, sending her falling back to the floor. Her head knocked into the corner of the couch. She winced and grabbed the back of her neck.

The music ended.

"What do you think you're doing? You could have killed someone!" Marcus glared at her from his place by her stereo. He held up the rolling pin he'd taken from her. "Why do you even have one of these? You don't cook."

"Mom bought it for me." She stood and winced, her hand going to her back. "Did you have to be so rough?"

"You were attacking me. It's instinct." Marcus sniffed the air. "Did you make popcorn?"

"It's in the microwave."

"Ooh!" Marcus wiggled his eyebrows and headed that way. "Sorry I scared you."

"Yeah, why are you so late?" Allie followed him to the kitchen and sat down on one of the island barstools, rubbing the back of her neck.

"Picked up another case."

"It was bad." She said knowingly.

Marcus nodded and put the bowl of popcorn between them, popping a piece in his mouth. "Kid came home from college to spend the weekend with his family and found his parents and sister dead."

Allie winced. "How?"

"Strangled with what looks like wire of some kind." Marcus pulled some curled up papers from his back pocket. "This reminds me, this is the case I promised you."

Allie snatched the papers from his hand and smoothed them out on the counter in front of her. "Another family?"

"Unfortunately. The fire marshal says it's homicide but I think he needs to go back and double check. Both of the Gilmore's were heavy smokers. They were older, smoke detectors never went off. It was just an accident."

"Did he say why he ruled it a homicide?"

Marcus popped a piece of popcorn in his mouth and shrugged. "Said the fire started in the bedroom and the Gilmore's bodies were found in the front room. To me, that means they tried to get out. They were in bed when the fire started, they woke up and tried to get out of the house and didn't make it."

Allie frowned and skimmed over the file. It made no sense. Marcus had a point. The Gilmore's hadn't been rich. They had no family, both retired from minimum wage jobs. "Where did they live? Anyone benefit from them being dead?"

"I couldn't find anything. They'd only lived in that house a few years. They moved there after they both retired." Marcus stuffed another handful of popcorn in his mouth. "I take it you agree with me. No motive for homicide."

Allie shook her head. "There has to be something else here." Biting her lip she read over the medical examiner's report again. They died from smoke inhalation. "No signs of a struggle?"

"Not that we could tell. The fire was pretty hot and took a while to put out. By the time they announced it homicide and we got on the scene, things were pretty much dissolved." Marcus chuckled. "And I mean that literally. The house was ash. It was an old house that lit up pretty quick."

Could a cigarette cause a fire like that? Allie had an uneasy feeling about this case. It didn't seem like homicide at all, but maybe that was exactly what they were supposed to think. What if the fire marshal was right?

"Was there anyone standing around watching the fire when you got there?"

"No, but like I said when we got there the fun was over." Marcus picked up a handful of popcorn. "What are you thinking?"

"I'm thinking maybe the fire marshal is right and it is homicide. While what you said makes sense, it doesn't add up."

"Who could have motive to kill two old people with a worthless house, no money and no family? It makes no sense. Give me a motive."

Allie shrugged. "Nate didn't need motive, but he killed people without thinking twice." Allie met his eyes.

"You think Nate did this?"

"No, of course not." Allie picked the papers up. "I'm just saying it's possible. Let's go talk in the front room. It's more comfortable and your pizza is on the coffee table."

"I'll grab a plate and be there in a minute."

Allie sat sideways on the couch, arching her legs in front of her. She read through the fire marshal's report again. She needed to go see this crime scene. She agreed with Marcus, there wasn't motive, but the fire marshal couldn't be mistaken, could he?

3

Her laughter echoed around him. Tony slipped his arm around her waist and pulled her close. "Jenna, let's get out of here. I'll take you home." He flashed his most flirtatious smile.

Jenna took the bait. "That sounds nice." She bit her lip and raised her eyebrows. She rotated her back to him and glanced over her shoulder to wink at him. Jenna sashayed across the room and got her wallet from her friend in the corner booth before she dodged her way across the dance floor and back into his arms. "Take me home, Daddy."

Tony chuckled and pushed the door open for her. "I don't know where your new apartment is." It was a lie. He knew everything about her. He knew she frequented this club, he knew she would be one to easily go home with a man she barely knew and he knew that if she let him into her house, she'd lock her dog in the spare bedroom so they could go about the apartment freely.

"It's not hard. In fact, it's probably the second easiest thing you'll do tonight." She stared at his lips, her tongue gliding across her top lip.

Tony pushed her against his car. The easiest thing he did tonight was gain her trust. She really should have made this a little harder. It was almost *too* easy. "This is my car." He bent slightly, his face at the edge of her low-cut blouse as he opened the car door for her. "After you, Jen."

"Thank you." She slid into the car and smiled up at him.

Tony closed the door and walked around the car shaking his head. This job was the easiest one yet. He glanced at his watch as he slid into the car. He was ahead of schedule. Glancing at Jenna he smiled. He could take his time.

*****

Allie ducked under the caution tape and looked around the house. The smell of smoke still lingered heavily in the room. What must it have been like to be trapped in this house when it was burning? The fire hot all around you, smoke assaulting your lungs until finally your body could no longer fight and you died. Allie shuddered and shook her head. Fires terrified her, always had. She needed to do her searching and get out of here.

She opened the file Marcus had given her and looked at some of the pictures. The fire marshal had condemned the house. It was unstable. Walking around in here probably wasn't the smartest thing, but she needed answers.

Gingerly, she stepped past the entry way and into the front room where the victims had been found. Allie looked at the front room photos. Both victims had been found near the door. Had they tried to get out? She frowned and looked around the room. The fire had originated in a closet in the bedroom.

Allie snuck back toward the bedroom. There was only one closet in the room and it was directly across from the foot of the bed. She went to stand by the remnants of the bed. "I'm sleeping and I wake up to the smoke alarm going off?" Allie glanced at the report. No fire alarms. "So what wakes me up? The smoke in the room? The noise of the fire?"

The Gilmore's had been in their seventies, but still they would have had time to get from their bedroom and out of the house. Neither of them had health problems that would have slowed them down. Allie went to the window and glanced at the report. Traces of accelerant were found near the window.

The dresser was near the window and there were burned bottles of hairspray nearby. The hairspray would have gone up quickly. It would have exploded when it got too hot. That would have been the accelerant found, no doubt. The fire would have burned further. The hairspray exploding could have awakened anyone. By that time the fire would have been getting pretty big. Neighbors could have seen it by this time. So why didn't the fire department get called? The bedroom was toward the back of the house, but surely someone would have seen it.

Marcus thought a cigarette had started the fire, but the report didn't specify a cigarette. Most house fires were caused by cigarettes and both of the Gilmore's had been smokers. But the fire started in the closet and it was doubtful a cigarette could have been left lit in the closet.

Allie continued along the wall until she got to the closet. She spotted some wire and knelt down to get a closer look. She slipped on a glove and picked up the piece. It was in the shape of a large square but one of the sides was missing.

Shaking her head, she looked back at the report. Nothing was mentioned about metal pieces inside the house. Allie put the wire down and moved on. The closet had been the central point. So if this fire had been set on purpose, the closet would have been a quick, easy place to start.

Allie knelt down and sifted through the ashes in the bottom of the closet. Frowning, she pulled out another piece of wire. Similar to the other. "What in the world is this?" Allie pulled several more pieces of wire out and set it in a pile. Total she'd found twenty-seven pieces of the wire. "What were you guys doing with all of this?" Allie pulled off her glove and reached for her phone. She dialed Marcus and waited.

"What business did Mr. Gilmore have?"

"He was retired."

"Yes, but from where?"

"The grocery store over on Jackson. Why?"

Allie frowned at the metal pieces. "I'm at the scene. I think you should come down here."

"What?" he exclaimed and groaned, his voice lowering to a whisper. "You aren't supposed to be there. First of all, you aren't cleared for active duty. Second, that house is condemned because it's not safe. Get out of that house. I'll come get you, but you get out now."

The phone beeped in her ear and she looked at it to see Marcus had hung up on her. Rolling her eyes, she slipped her glove back on and picked up the wire. "He seriously needs to chill. It's not like I've never been to a crime scene before." She mumbled and shuffled to the door.

Halfway to the entry way she stopped and glanced into the kitchen. She looked at the floor. It seemed safe enough. It would take Marcus at least ten minutes to get there. She could look around just a little bit longer. Biting her lip, she snuck back to the kitchen. There she found the remnants of whiskey, vodka and tequila bottles. The Gilmore's didn't seem the type to have so much hard alcohol on hand.

Side-stepping a soft spot on the floor, she continued to search the room with her eyes. Above the kitchen there was a melted smoke alarm. Why hadn't the smoke alarm gone off? Stepping back over to the door, she stood up on her toes to reach the alarm. It was melted to the wall. She gave it a tug and it wouldn't budge.

Groaning, she set the wires and file on the floor and reached back up for the smoke alarm. "Come on you stupid thing." She jerked it as hard as she could and it popped loose. Allie gasped, losing her balance and falling.

The floor crumbled beneath her. She dropped the alarm and covered her head as the whole floor started caving like dominos. The old kitchen island began to teeter. Allie curled up in a ball, bracing for the impact.

The island landed with a crash, crumbling against her side. Allie screamed in pain as a hard object stabbed into her side. Smoke and ash blew up around her and she coughed, gasping for air. She tried to move, to wiggle out, but the pain in her side intensified. Marcus would never let her hear the end of this.

Allie tried to reach the phone in her back pocket but she couldn't move her arm. She was stuck. Her only hope was that Marcus would get there soon and come in to yell at her. If Ashton found out about this, she would no doubt be on desk duty for the rest of her career. She coughed, her chest burning. *Marcus, please hurry.*

*****

Marcus pulled up and saw Allie's car. He parked behind it and walked up to the driver's side. She wasn't in the car. Marcus sighed, put his hands on his hips and looked at the house. "That woman is never going to learn." He went over to the front door and poked his head into the house. "Allie?" He called.

"Marcus! Marcus I'm stuck."

"You're stuck?" He exclaimed and ducked into the house. "Where are you?" He stopped when he saw the badly burned floor. How had she walked on this floor? Surely it couldn't hold that much weight.

"I'm in the kitchen." She gasped and started coughing.

Marcus shook his head. "You're going to be the death of me, you know that?"

"I know. I'm sorry." She coughed again.

Marcus took slow steady breaths, willing the floorboards to hold him. He saw the hole in the kitchen floor. Allie must be in the hole. How was he supposed to get her out? One of the cabinets had fallen over on her. "Are you hurt? Can you move at all?"

"No, this thing is on me and I can't move. My side hurts." She cried.

Marcus winced, getting as close to the edge of the hole as he dared. "All right, well I'm going to see if I can get down in this hole with you and lift the cabinet. I see your legs and it looks like the only part pinning you down is the countertop. When you feel it give, try to get free."

"Okay."

Marcus jumped down in the hole, straddling her legs. He mentally measured the size of the cabinet. He could lift this. It was no different than the weights at the gym. Squatting down, he gripped the edge of the cabinet. "All right, Al. On the count of three. Ready?"

"Yes."

"One, two, three." Marcus grunted and pushed the cabinet up with all the strength he could muster. He felt like it barely budged. "Anything?"

"I can move a little bit." Allie grunted.

"Oof! I'm on my back now. Lift it just a little higher."

"Easy for you to say!" Marcus grunted and pushed harder. His arms started quivering. "What did they keep in this cabinet? Gold bars?"

"I'm out!"

Marcus let the cabinet drop. He leaned against it panting. He glanced over at Allie's dirt smudged, tear-streaked face and shook his head. "Why don't you ever listen?"

"Where's the fun in that?" Allie stood up and winced, grasping her side.

"You're bleeding." Marcus went to her side and lifted the edge of her shirt to see a large cut. "You're going to need stitches. Let's get you to the hospital."

"In a minute. Look what I found." Allie leaned over the cabinet and pulled out the wires, passing them over to him.

"What are they?" he asked taking them from her.

"I have no idea but I found about twenty of them in the closet."

"This could be the key to everything." Marcus held up the wire square and shook his head back and forth. "This could be the answer to everything, Allie. I'm so glad you risked your life. It will be so worth it!"

Allie narrowed her eyes at him. "Really? I could do without your sarcasm."

Marcus chuckled and tossed the wire aside. "You're barking up the wrong tree, Al. I think it's from the blood loss." Marcus climbed from the hole and held his hand out to help her. "Let's get you to the hospital. Obviously giving you that case file was a bad idea."

Allie groaned as he pulled her up out of the hole. "It wasn't a bad idea. Getting a fresh set of eyes is always good. Didn't you tell me that?"

"Yes, but a fresh set of eyes that's delusional, that's not good." Marcus searched the floor to avoid weak spots as they made their way to the front door

"Come on now, Marc. Don't be ridiculous."

"I have two new cases to deal with and I can't keep leaving work to bail you out so it has to end here." Marcus bent over and stretched his back. The muscles tightened and he turned to either side to massage the muscles. He straightened and sighed. "I'll get the case file from you tonight."

"You have two new cases? Are they connected to this one?"

"No, because I don't think this one should even be mine." Marcus glanced over at Allie. He knew that look on her face. She wanted in on the cases. "No."

"Marcus, please. I promise I won't go anywhere I'm not supposed to. I'm going crazy not having anything to do and you *know* I can help you with this."

"What about your psych eval? You haven't passed it. If someone finds out I gave you these cases, I could be in a lot trouble." Marcus shook his head. "It's not happening."

Allie huffed and spun on her heel to go to her car.

"Where are you going?"

"Home."

Marcus rolled his eyes and followed after her. "You can't go home, you need to go to the hospital and get that cut stitched up." He hurried over to her car and slammed the door shut just as she started to open it. He leaned against the door, his face inches from hers. "Please. Let me take you to the hospital."

"I just want to help with the case."

"I know." Marcus pushed away from the car and ran his hand through his hair. "All right, I'll let you look at them and do whatever you want, but I have to be there."

Allie's eyes locked with his. "Are you serious?"

Going against his better judgment, he nodded. "I'll bring the files tonight."

"Thank you!" Allie squealed, throwing her arms around his neck. The embrace lasted half a second before her hands dropped to her side. "Okay, take me to the hospital now." She moaned and limped to his car.

Marcus shook his head and followed after her. He had to keep track of her and make sure she didn't do any more crazy stunts like this one. He should be getting paid extra for this.

4

"Come on in, Allie. Close the door." Dr. Seaver stood as she entered the room and stepped forward to shake her hand. "Did you have a good week?"

"Yes. Can we get this over with? I have a lot of work to do." Allie sat down in one of the chairs across from him and leaned back, crossing her legs.

"You haven't taken any of these sessions seriously and it concerns me."

"Just let me get back to my job. That's all I want!" Allie uncrossed her legs and leaned forward, resting her elbows on her knees. "What do I have to do to pass this? It's been a month. Do you always torture people this long? You're giving me a problem I should probably see another psychiatrist about."

"You think I want to keep you here? Captain Ashton wants me to make sure you aren't going to lose your cool out there and seriously hurt yourself or someone else. Everyone seems a little hesitant where you're concerned. No one wants to work with you."

His words were like a knife to the stomach. "Marcus would work with me."

"Marcus is the exception because he fancies himself in love with you."

Allie scoffed. "Whatever, doc." She sat back in the chair, crossing her legs again. "Well start with the questioning."

"You're favoring your right side. What happened?"

"Stitches. I fell and cut my side." Allie looked over at him, holding her hand out to stop his next question. "It was just an accident and Marcus was there, you can ask him. He took me to the hospital."

Dr. Seaver nodded. "Are you all right?"

Allie narrowed her eyes at him. What angle was he playing? "Yes, I'm fine. The stitches didn't feel too good and they're still tight but I'm getting used to them."

"That's good." He sighed and stood up, sauntering over to his desk. "I've been debating as of late, not knowing what I should do with you."

"Letting me go would be a good start."

"That's what I thought." His smile seemed forced. "Coming in here every week isn't doing you any good. You're bitter and prideful and you don't think anything can help you. So, I'm giving you this release."

Dr. Seaver held up a sealed white envelope. The envelope practically glowed. It was her gold ticket. "What's the catch?" Her eyes still locked on the envelope.

He came around his desk and held the envelope out to her. Her fingers closed around it, but he didn't let go. "There isn't a catch, really. All I'm asking is when the time comes, you come to me. That's all."

"Fine." She tugged at the envelope but he still gripped it tightly. She met his eyes. "Let it go."

Dr. Seaver shook his head. "Promise me you'll come back when the time comes."

Allie rolled her eyes. "Fine. If and when the time comes, I promise I will come back."

The forced smile cracked his face once more. "Perfect. Stay safe, Allie." His fingers released the envelope.

She stared at him for a moment, then stood up and left the office before he could change his mind. Once out of the office, she leaned against the wall and breathed a sigh of relief. Finally, she was free from the head-shrinker.

Allie pulled her cell phone from her pocket and dialed Marcus as she made her way out of the hospital. "Hey, I'm on my way back to the precinct."

"Session ended early, huh?"

"No, I'm done! I have my release in my hand right now." Allie couldn't contain her excitement, not with Marcus.

"Really?"

Allie scoffed. "Come on, don't sound so skeptical. I'm unarmed."

"Right, meaning you don't have a gun, but we both know you can be very convincing in many other ways."

She could hear the smile in his voice and she shook her head. "You're ridiculous. The doctor is still in once piece. No bruises, broken bones or cuts on his person."

"That's good to know. Congratulations. Glad you've finally decided to stop slacking off and come back to work. Now I don't have to worry about getting in trouble for giving you case files."

"I won't forget that. I'm ready to get started. I still want to run down that wire I found at the Gilmore's house."

"Allie, really? What makes you think that wire means anything? We have two other cases to work on. Give it up."

Allie pursed her lips and slid into her car.

"I'm not going to give up. Two people are dead and the only thing out of sorts with the whole house was that wire."

"Well in the other cases there are people dead too. The Lancaster's were strangled, four of them. Then there's this new case with a college girl, Jenna. You can't tell me they don't deserve justice as well."

Allie sighed. "They do."

"All right, then there's no point in looking at a cold case that probably isn't even murder but a wayward cigarette. We need to focus on what obviously is murder."

She didn't want to give up the Gilmore's case. She could work with Marcus on the other cases and he wouldn't think twice about giving her the Gilmore's case file to work on after hours. She could make some headway with that. "Fine. I'll be there soon. When I get done talking to Ashton, I need to get my gun back and then I'll be ready to start."

"It'll be lunch time by then. How about we meet for lunch at the café about 12:30? I can fill you in on the cases and we can get this ball rolling."

"Sounds good. Did Ashton give you anyone to work with on these assignments?"

"Yeah, he is having me work with Megan Hiddleston. She's still a little wet behind the ears and of *no* help to me whatsoever. She actually threw up when she went into the Lancaster's house."

"Well, not everyone has a strong stomach and if it's her first case, give her a break. In fact, bring her along with you to lunch. I want to meet her." Allie heard Marcus' sigh and reluctant agreement. She hung up with him and started her car. Megan may be new to this, but everyone started out new and she had to do better with this protégé than she did with the last one.

5

Allie sat down at her computer and pulled up a search browser. "This is stupid." She mumbled, yet still typed the words 'images wire square' into the search bar. "All right, show me something, please." All that came up were pictures of sunglasses and a few of Ethan Hunt from Mission Impossible. But this wasn't Mission Impossible.

"What are you looking for?" Megan sat down in the chair by her desk and frowned at her computer screen. "Are you buying new sunglasses?"

Allie sighed. "No, I'm trying to figure out what these wire things we found at the Gilmore's house were."

"I thought Marcus said that case was cold."

"He thinks it is, but I don't."

Megan nodded. "Well maybe I could help. Do you have the wire thing with you?"

"No, Marcus made me leave them behind after he made fun of me. He's also forbidden me to go back into the house." Allie looked over at Megan. Marcus hadn't forbidden Megan to go into the house. She mentally shook the thought away. This is precisely the type of sticky situation she would get her protégé into and end up getting her killed, just like she had Carly.

"I could probably get them for you. Where in the house were they?"

"No, you probably shouldn't go in. The house really isn't stable after the fire. I think they'll be demolishing it soon."

"More reason for us to act quickly. Come on, how hard could it be to get in there, grab the wire and come out? It'd take me all of five minutes, if that."

Megan was very convincing. If Marcus found out she allowed Megan to go in there she'd be in a heap of trouble though. "No, Megan. It's best not to." Allie furrowed her brow in thought. "However, we could go to the other crime scenes and maybe we could see if the wire is found anywhere in their homes."

"Road trip?" The corner of Megan's mouth hitched up in a smile.

"Road trip." Allie smiled and grabbed her keys from her desk drawer. "Where is Marcus?"

"In Ashton's office."

Allie glanced that way. Both men were laughing about something. "I'll go check if he wants to come along. Meet me by the elevator." Allie went over to the office and rapped on the door before poking her head inside. "Megan and I are heading to the Lancaster's. Did you want to come?"

"Why are you going there?" Marcus stood and handed her a file. "This is everything we found on scene."

Allie tucked the file under her arm. "Thanks, but I want to look for myself. You know that."

Marcus sighed and nodded. "Fine. I'll stick around here for a while. I'm still verifying Jenna's timeline."

"Suit yourself." Allie closed the door and met Megan at the elevator. "He's gonna wait here. That will give us plenty of time to search both scenes." The women stepped into the elevator and pushed the button for the parking garage. "Tell me what you know about the Lancaster's."

Megan took a deep breath and started. "All we know right now is they were having a family barbeque and it appears they were just sitting down to eat when they were attacked. The children were both killed quickly, broken necks. The father and mother were both strangled with what appears to be wire. They had a son in college and he came home and found them. We found footprints on the scene that didn't match the college son or the father. Boot print size 12."

"Big feet." The elevator chimed and the doors opened. "He killed the children quickly. He didn't really want to do it. How old were the children?"

"Ten and six."

Allie nodded slid behind the wheel of her car. "All right, what about Jenna."

"We are still verifying her last few hours but from what we have learned, she was at a night club. She hit it off with some guy and left with him. She was going to college here in town."

"Any relationship with the Lancaster's son?"

Megan frowned. "I don't know. I didn't think about it. Marcus may have. I'll have to ask him when we get back."

Allie pulled out on the street and handed a file to Megan. "Here. Marcus gave me this. Read through it and let me know if there is anything different in there than what you told me just now. Specifically look at the college kid. See if there is a connection between him and Jenna."

The car was silent as Megan read through the case file. Allie took the time to think about the cases. Everything was happening so fast. If she'd been on scene with Marcus at all of these, she would have a much better idea of what they were doing. She didn't like reading someone else's work. She preferred to do her own searching. She didn't trust people to be as thorough as she was.

There had to be some connection between the three cases. The cases were stacking up fast, but so far there were no similarities between the victims. She had a gut feeling though and she always trusted her gut.

"It doesn't say here that they knew each other but they went to the same school. We could set up a time to talk to him about it." Megan folded the file and pulled out her phone. "I think I still have his number here."

"What was his name?"

"Ben. He's eighteen, still lives at home, no girlfriend."

"Where is he staying at right now?"

"He was in a hotel room. Should I call him?"

"Yeah, see if he can meet us at the precinct in about an hour." Allie pulled into the driveway of the Lancaster's house. "I'm going inside. Come in when you get off the phone."

Megan nodded and greeted the person on the phone.

Allie took the case file and walked up to the front porch. She took a deep breath and ducked under the caution tape. She unlocked the door and stepped inside. Everything was still a mess. A fight obviously broke out. Allie closed the door and turned to look at it.

Someone knocks on their door. First thing she would do is look to see who it was. There wasn't a peephole but there were narrow windows on either side of the door. She pulled the curtain back and looked. If she saw someone who didn't seem menacing, but you didn't know who they were, you wouldn't immediately open the door.

Unless you were a man. Men weren't as cautious about such things. Or a child might not be.

But judging by the time of death, it's unlikely the children would be answering the door. Parents would surely know better than to have their child answer the door so late at night.

Allie opened the door and swung it back and forth, testing the hinges. They were loose. The killer pushed their way into the house. Allie turned around and noted the broken table behind the door. They pushed their way in, knocking the father back onto the table and breaking it.

The door opened and Megan poked her head inside. "It took some convincing but he said he would meet us. I doubt he'll want to stick around long. I know he's still pretty shaken up."

Allie nodded. "Good job. Come in and close the door."

"What are you doing?"

"I'm looking to see what happened." Allie pointed at the broken table. "Killer forces his way inside, breaks the table."

"Right. First thing he'd want to do is subdue Mr. Lancaster."

Allie smiled. "And why is that?"

"He's the strongest. He would be the hardest to control so you'd want to get control of him first. If you were to attack his wife or the children, he could easily stop you or even kill you before you did what you came to do. And with this being his house, he'd have every right. The mother is more likely to protect her children than to fight for her husband. And he'd want her to do that."

"You're exactly right. Good job." Allie patted Megan on the back. "So now, how did he subdue Mr. Lancaster?"

"He could have had a gun."

Allie nodded. "He could have, but at this point, wouldn't you throw caution to the wind and just take a chance. This man is obviously here to kill you anyway."

"Right. Um, well Mr. Lancaster was beaten. It's possible they got into an altercation." Megan motioned to the front room. "It also explains the turned over coffee table and the broken pictures."

"Indeed." Allie looked around the room. "If you were Mr. Lancaster, how would you defend yourself?"

"Well, as a man, if they were about the same size, he'd probably just charge him and take his chances. I imagine it was more of a fist fight."

"Okay, so if it was, they would have been fighting awhile, right? Why didn't Mrs. Lancaster leave?"

Megan looked over at the dining room. "They were sitting down to eat. Maybe they did leave."

"Where were the bodies found?"

"At the dining room table. They were all sitting in their chairs. They were all tied up and gagged."

"Tied up with what?"

"Zip ties, behind the back. They were cinched tight enough to break the skin on all of them."

"So by the time he got them tied, he was angry." Allie looked at the autopsy photos. "They were all strangled."

"The children didn't appear to be but we don't have the autopsy back on them. Dana is running behind. At first glance she said there weren't any signs of bruising."

"It can take a few days for that to show up. She probably hasn't had a chance for that though." Allie shook her head. "He should have been able to subdue Mr. Lancaster fairly easily. He wears a size 12. He has to be a large man."

"And Mr. Lancaster was average height and weight. Ben is very timid and I suspect his father was the same way. So maybe they fight a little bit, but maybe the fight didn't last long enough for Mrs. Lancaster to make her escape."

Allie nodded. "So he gets Lancaster tied to the chair. He orders the children and Mrs. Lancaster to sit down." Allie walked over to the dining table and stood at the head of the table. "Who does he kill first?"

"The children."

Allie glanced over her shoulder at Megan. "Why the children?"

"Because he killed them quickly. He didn't want them to suffer. Naturally, he'd kill them first so they didn't have to suffer with seeing their parents killed in front of them."

"He kills the children. Next, he kills Mrs. Lancaster."

"Why?"

"Because he is attacking Mr. Lancaster. He wants him to suffer the most."

"Why do you say that?"

Allie shook her head. "I don't know. It's just a feeling."

Megan smiled. "Marcus told me about you and your gut feelings. He said to always trust them."

"My gut hasn't failed me yet." Allie closed the case file and sighed.

"Now what?"

"We check the house. I want to check the garage first." Allie headed for the door.

"Why the garage? Nothing happened in there." Megan hurried after her.

"If I'm right and that wire I found at the Gilmore's means something, then the Lancaster's will have it too." Allie opened the garage door and they began their search. The Gilmore's wires had been found in a closet. So the wires weren't something that would be used often. Allie checked her watch. They only had about fifteen minutes before they needed to go back to the precinct to meet Ben. "Megan, you find anything?"

"No. You?"

"Nothing. Let's check the house. We only have fifteen minutes." Allie went back into the house and first thing she checked were the closets. There were no wires anywhere. Maybe Marcus was right and she was barking up the wrong tree.

Allie and Megan locked up the house and made their way back to the precinct. "I'm sorry. I really thought we'd find something." Megan sounded very disappointed.

"Sometimes you don't find anything because what you're looking at doesn't make sense. We were looking for those wires and they weren't there, but maybe there was something else we were missing."

"There wasn't a lot to see in there, though. I mean, the only thing that really stood out was a stack of flyers for the mayoral campaign."

"Why did that stand out?"

"They were flyers for Dan Norton." Megan said simply and shrugged. "I didn't think anyone liked Dan Norton anymore."

"Oh you'd be surprised. A lot of people are standing behind him because of Kent Bradley. They may not agree with what Dan Norton has done the past few years, but they certainly don't want to know what could happen if Kent Bradley gets in there."

"That's true. Slim pickings this time around, isn't it?"

Allie laughed and nodded. "Every time, if you ask me. I'm not the biggest fan of politicians, especially the mayor who ends up being our boss."

"Good point." Megan turned in her seat to look at Allie. "Could I ask you a question?"

"Shoot."

"Are you and Marcus together?"

"Wow! That was a quick change of subject." Allie laughed and glanced over at her. "Why do you ask?"

"Oh, he just talks about you all the time. He just seems to really like you."

First her psychiatrist and now Megan. "Marcus and I are just friends. We have a mutual respect for each other. That's all."

Megan sighed, shaking her head. "If you say so. I don't think he'd agree, though."

Allie glanced over at Megan and then looked back at the road. This was all just rumor. Megan was new and no doubt someone was messing with her.

Allie and Marcus had been friends for a few years now. There was no way he would sit by and let a friendship continue when he wanted more. Marcus wanted action, not waiting. Although, he did talk about her wall a lot. Maybe he wasn't sure how to scale the wall. No. They were friends, but what if she asked Marcus about it tonight?

6

"What is Ben Lancaster doing here?"

Marcus sat down on the edge of Allie's desk.

"Don't tell me you made that poor kid come down here for more questions."

"I did. I have some more questions for him."

"Like what, if he had any wire squares?"

"Maybe."

Marcus rolled his eyes. "Megan told me you had her looking for them at the Lancaster house. You're not going to give this up, are you?"

"You don't know I'm wrong until you prove otherwise." Allie sat back in her chair and crossed her legs. "Megan said she would question Ben for me. She's also going to ask him about Jenna Cortland."

"What about her?"

"They went to the same school. It's possible they know each other. If they don't then I'll look for something else."

Marcus crossed his arms over his chest and shook his head. "Why are you so convinced all of these cases are connected?"

Allie sighed and sat up, spreading the files out on her desk. "What are the odds that there are three separate murders in the same town, about a week apart from each other and there is *no* connection?"

"All right, they were all killed in different ways. Evidence shows that Jenna was single, but someone had stayed over at her house that night, most likely the guy she met at the club. None of the others have a similar story like that. You have three different types of people being killed. An older couple who smokes multiple packs a day, a family of five where one member is left standing, and a single young college girl. There are no similarities. Killers have types."

"Nate didn't have a type."

Marcus rolled his eyes. "Yes, and he is the exception to every rule." He stood up and paced over to his desk. "I thought we agreed not to bring him up anymore."

"I guess I don't get why it bothers you so much. Is it because he was my friend? I'm not limited to just one friend, Marc, I can have several." Allie slapped the files up in a stack. "Get rid of this stupid jealous attitude of yours and be serious about our work."

"I'm not jealous! The man was a *killer*, Allie! What part of that don't you understand?"

"He was nice. And him being a killer isn't the whole story."

"You're right, because he was also a sneaky thief who likes to lock people in bathrooms!" Marcus sat down, jaw clenched. "I can't believe you're still defending him."

Allie leaned forward and glanced around them, her voice just above a whisper. "Do you remember nothing of what I told you about the visit in the hospital? He said he only killed the people he was told to kill."

"Right, so that makes killing people okay. Sorry, I guess I missed that." Marcus snapped his fingers and pointed at Allie. "That's it! Maybe we should tell him to kill this murderer we've been chasing. Nate can find the guy and put an end to this for good."

"You're so childish, you know that? There is something to what Nate said. Someone is pulling his strings and making him do these things. They're probably blackmailing him."

"You don't know that for sure. And if you think these cases are all connected, what makes you so sure Nate isn't the one killing these people as well?"

"He wouldn't kill children. Besides that, fire, strangulation, and suffocation are not his style. He's an executioner whose weapon of choice is a handgun."

"And a knife."

He saw Allie's jaw tighten. "He didn't do that. Mrs. Meek confessed and it was proven she stabbed Katie."

"Yes, after Nate shot her in the head."

Allie stood up and pushed her chair in, snatching up her files. "I'm done discussing this with you. When we do find Nate, I'll prove to you right then and there that he is a good man and you'll see that I was right this whole time."

"I look forward to that day so I can rub it in your face that I'm right." Marcus watched her storm to the interrogation room. She would get over her anger fast, she usually did. He probably shouldn't have argued with her, especially about Nate. She'd been very sensitive about it the past few weeks. Some day he hoped she would see that Nate was nothing more than a killer who deserved life in prison or death.

Marcus checked his watch. It was time for his meeting. He stuck his head into Ashton's office to let him know he was going and then jogged to the elevator. He stepped in and pushed the garage button, staring at the numbers as they took him down to the basement level. Marcus got in his car and headed to the state prison.

The drive was becoming too familiar to him. He didn't want to spend his days going out to the prison, but until he got the answers he was searching for, he refused to stop going. One day he would learn everything he needed to know.

He walked into the prison and signed his name on the visitor list.

"Good afternoon, Marcus. How's life on the outside."

"About the same as always." Marcus forced a smile. "How are you doing, Gary."

"Still here. You seeing him again today?"

"Yeah."

"I figured. He's in there waiting for you."

Marcus gave a curt nod and started down the hall to the visitor's room he always used. The guard opened the door, revealing the prisoner sitting at the table with a smug smile on his face. Marcus made fists with his hands and stuffed them in his pocket to keep from punching the guy.

"Well, well, Detective Marcus. Good to see you again. How about a game of chess?"

Marcus pulled the chair out opposite the prisoner. "I'm not here to play games, Bastian. Tell me what I want to know."

*****

Allie walked up to Jenna Cortland's apartment and stopped at the door. What had Jenna been doing right before she was killed. Marcus said she brought a guy home. Did she know the guy? Had she trusted him and he had betrayed her? She knew what that was like. She'd trusted Nate and he'd turned her over to her worst nightmare. Allie was thankful her circumstances hadn't ended the way Jenna's had.

"Everything okay?" Megan raised her eyebrows and looked at the door. "You brought the key, right?"

Allie shook her head. "Yeah, of course. Here." She handed over the key with the lucky rabbit foot keychain dangling from it. Luck had not been Jenna's friend that night.

Megan unlocked the door and went inside. "This is a pretty small apartment, not much to see here."

"Did Ben have anything to say about Jenna? Did he know her?"

"No. He said he'd seen her on campus because she was doing a campus campaign for Dan Norton. He said her and her group was always handing out flyers at the mall or somewhere. Said from what he'd heard around campus, she was a little obsessed."

Allie nodded. "You know, more people support that guy than I ever thought would." She shrugged and looked around the front room and kitchen. "This is a tiny apartment. What year was Jenna?"

"Second year. She was getting a degree in political science. After that, her plan was law school."

"She had big dreams." Allie sighed and walked back toward the bedroom. "She was killed in the bedroom, right?"

"Yes, on the bed."

Allie stepped into the room and her mouth dropped open. There were campaign posters cluttering up every wall. She had t-shirts, hats, signs, extra signs and flyers, all with Dan Norton's smiling face and his slogan 'Committed to Great' stamped across them. "This is unbelievable. To say she was a little obsessed is an understatement."

"I'll say. Do you think he killed her?"

Allie frowned. "Dan Norton? The guy can barely put a sentence together, let alone a murder plot."

"Point taken."

"Where are Jenna's parents?"

"Both dead. She was orphaned when she was six. She was passed through the foster care system for eleven years before she was adopted by a woman here in town. The woman died two years ago."

"So Jenna had nobody."

"Pretty much."

Allie shook her head and continued to look around the room. "Who was she with at the club last night?"

"A friend." Megan pulled her phone out and flipped through a list. "Haylee Jameson."

"You keep all your notes on your phone?"

Megan nodded. "Why not? I always have it with me."

"Phones can lose battery, get stolen or get broken. It's best to have a written copy too."

"All of my notes are transferred from my phone to my cloud drive so I can access them anywhere." Megan smiled. "I prefer the electronics to the old fashion stuff."

A small part of her died inside. She was old fashion. Megan basically just told her she was old. Shaking her head, she put it behind her and focused on the case. She saw a picture on the dresser and went to look at it. It was of Jenna and an older woman. "Her adopted mom?"

"Yes."

"What do we know about her mom?"

Megan sighed and flipped to another page on her phone. "Widow. Her husband had been killed in the terrorist attack back in 2001. She never remarried. She grew up around here and moved back after he died. She got money from her husband's life insurance and was able to live off that. She adopted Jenna three years ago. Ten years to the day of her husband's death. She must have been lonely."

Allie nodded. "Was she a Dan Norton supporter as well?"

"I don't know." Megan frowned. "Why does it matter?"

"Jenna got this obsession from somewhere. It's one thing to support a candidate. This," Allie motioned around the room. "This is madness."

"I'll make a note of it and check later."

Allie continued around the room and stopped at the bedside table. Something was sticking out from under the bed. Allie frowned and knelt down, slipping her gloves on before pulling a messenger bag out from under the bed. It was heavy. "Megan, come here."

Megan was at her side in an instant, pulling on a pair of gloves. "How could they have missed this before?"

"A lot can be overlooked when you're only focused on one thing." Allie opened the bag and pulled out some files. She started flipping through the papers. She stopped when she saw the letterhead of Dan Norton. "Wow! Do you know what this is?" She handed the paper to Megan.

"This is the mayor's!" Megan's eyes grew large as she read the paper. "These are his financials." Megan picked up another paper. "This is basically all of his campaign information."

Allie shook her head. "Makes me wonder what kind of stuff Jenna was into."

"Why didn't Mayor Norton report a break in?"

"He's the type to do his own investigating. Let's go have a chat with the mayor."

"I'll call Marcus and have him meet us there."

Allie nodded and slipped the files back in the bag. Megan took the bag with her as she headed out the door and called Marcus. Allie continued her walk around the room. She opened the closet door and frowned at the dart board on the back of the door. Mayor Norton's face was on the bulls-eye. Something wasn't right. Allie walked over to the posters on the wall and peeled back the corner of one. Behind it was a poster for Kent Bradley. Her hands shook as she pulled out her phone and snapped a picture.

Jenna had been playing both sides of the game. Someone must have found out. Allie pocketed her phone and hurried out to join Megan. She jogged down the steps. After pushing through the outer door, she pulled her phone back out to check the time. It was just after one so hopefully the mayor would be in his office. As she rounded the corner to get to the car, she saw Megan lying unconscious next to the car.

7

Marcus rushed across the parking lot and through the automatic doors. Allie paced the waiting room. "What happened?"

Allie shook her head. "I don't know yet. She's in surgery." Allie's lips were tight, her arms crossed over her chest.

"Are you all right?"

"No, Marc. I'm not all right." She sighed and paced away from him, her hands on her hips. She stopped and spun around to face him, two fingers held up in the air. "Two minutes! She left to call you and she was gone maybe two minutes before I joined her. How did this happen?"

"Al, this isn't your fault."

"Right, sure. She worked with you for months and nothing like this happened, the one day she works with me and she gets stabbed." Allie shook her head and continued her pacing. "Someone knew we found that bag, but how?"

"What was in the bag?"

"Financials for the mayor's campaign. The only person who could want that is Kent Bradley." Allie shook her head. "But I don't see him stabbing someone, or even hiring someone to do it."

Marcus frowned and sat down in one of the chairs. "Jenna's room was covered with posters for Dan Norton but I checked with the mayor's campaign manager and he has no record of Jenna working for them."

"Then how did she get her hands on those papers?" Allie shook her head. "And look at this." She pulled out her cell phone and handed it to him.

Marcus shook his head at the Kent Bradley poster and handed the phone back to her. "You don't think Jenna is playing both sides, do you?"

"I don't know. We could go talk to Kent Bradley and find out if he knew Jenna. It makes me wonder about the timing of her death. Those records were in a messenger bag under her bed. Jenna was killed in her bedroom, but you said a witness showed her going into her apartment with a man, right?"

"Right. According to her neighbor, the guy looked way too old for her, but Jenna was too drunk to care." Marcus shrugged. "This person wouldn't have been after those papers. The apartment hadn't been searched. Whoever killed her was there just to kill her and nothing more."

"Unless he got caught up in the moment and forgot."

Marcus scoffed. "Yeah, I doubt that. Don't you remember how anal Nate was? He picked pieces of dirt from his clothes that you couldn't see with a microscope. A hired killer pays attention to detail. It's his job. He doesn't forget things like that."

"You're right. So whoever killed her didn't care about the papers. It is a great motive though." Allie snapped and sat down next to him. "Okay, what if they had Jenna killed because they found out she stole the papers. Maybe they thought that Jenna had already taken the papers to Kent Bradley and only just realized that wasn't the case."

Marcus shook his head. "It's thin, Allie. Their first assumption would be that Jenna still had the papers."

"All depends on when they went missing."

Marcus nodded and stood up. "Let's go talk to Mayor Norton and then we'll go have a chat with Mr. Bradley."

"What about Megan? I have to stay until she's out of surgery."

"Then I'll go talk to Bradley and stop back by before I go to the mayor's office." Marcus pulled his phone out. "It's two-thirty. The mayor may have to wait until tomorrow."

Allie grinned. "Or we could inconvenience him."

"Do you know how much trouble he could cause? Ashton would never forgive you." Marcus chuckled and shook his head. "It would be funny, though. I'll give you a call when I'm on my way back from Bradley's office."

Allie nodded and stood up, glancing around. "Watch your back. Something isn't right here. I don't want two partners in the hospital."

Marcus made a fist and hit his chest twice. "You can't hurt steel."

Allie laughed and pushed him toward the door. "Get out of here."

"Catch you later." He walked outside and stopped. He'd had a squad car drop him off. Marcus went back in. "I need to take your car. I was dropped off."

"Bring it back in one piece." Allie dug the keys from her pocket and tossed them to him.

Marcus searched the lot for the car. He headed towards it, pulling his phone out to call Kent Bradley's campaign office. He stopped and leaned against the car as he talked to the secretary. He hung up and he pushed the unlock button. The car chirped once before it exploded.

*****

People shouldn't be allowed to drive such fancy cars. It just made them think they were better than everyone else. His brother was among those stuck up pigs. His parents had been that way as well. Things hadn't ended well for them.

Glancing at the auto handbook, he frowned at the drawing. "I thought this was supposed to be easy to understand." He grumbled and flipped back to the table of contents. He scratched his head with his knife as he skimmed through the chapter headings.

Brakes. He sighed and shook his head. "The brakes are operated using a hydraulic system." He mocked. "That's great, but where is this hydraulic system?"

A noise behind him caught his attention and he ducked quickly and glanced around. He took slow deep breaths through his mouth in an attempt to keep quiet. Light laughter grew closer and closer. Biting his lip, he slipped his knife into his pocket and crawled around to the other side of the van. Tony resting his back against the front driver's side tire. He closed his eyes, hoping the couple wouldn't see him and question.

Their voices got closer and stopped.

"Someone left their hood up." The man said.

"Maybe they're in the car." The woman said. "Come on, let's go. It's late."

"Now hold on, maybe they need help."

He winced and lay flat on his back, hoping he could squeeze under the car. Footsteps got louder as they inched their way around the van. His shirt caught on the edge of the van and he closed his eyes as his shirt ripped. The separating of the fabric seemed to echo in the stillness of the night.

"Hey, do you need some help, sir?" The man asked kneeling down next to him.

He cleared his throat. "Nah, just finishing up. Took a lot longer to replace than I thought. Those manuals are no help when doing real repairs."

The man chuckled. "I understand that. My brother is a mechanic. I could see if he could stop by and check it out."

"No!" He cleared his throat. "Sorry. No thank you. I've got it now."

"All right. Well, good luck, sir." He tapped the side of the car and the couple went on their way. Tony rested his head against the warm asphalt. "Keep it together, Tony." He mumbled and dug his phone out of his pocket. He used the backlight to see where his shirt was caught. One little nut was all it took to rip a hole the size of a small child in his shirt.

Shaking his head he unhooked his shirt from the nut. He started to shimmy out from under the car and stopped. "Duh, I can do this down here."

Pulling the knife from his pocket, he held his phone up to the tires and searched for the brake line.

Tony sawed into the line. It didn't take long for fluid to seep from the line. His nose scrunched as the foul smell reached him. It wouldn't take long for the fluid to drain from the line. They probably make it to the interstate when the brakes went out.

Perfect timing.

Shimmying out from under the car, he ducked under the bumper and chiseled into the brake line in the rear of the car as well. He may as well do his job thoroughly. He hesitated momentarily, eying the gas tank. No, the breaks would be better than the gas. Gas was too easy.

With both lines severed, he crawled out from under the car and gathered up his tools. He closed the hood and locked the car back before jogging back to his car parked a block away. Tony sat behind the wheel and picked up the notebook on the seat next to him. He crossed off the Albright's. His next stop would be the Prescott's. Could he manage two in one week? Probably.

Settling back in his seat, he set the alarm on his phone for 7 o'clock when the Albright's would leave for work. He would hate to miss the big show.

8

Allie marched up the steps and flashed her badge as she went through the doors. "I have an appointment." She announced and continued on to the office at the end of the hall. She jerked the door open and went inside.

The secretary stood up and came around the desk. "Mayor Norton isn't accepting visitors today."

"He's accepting this one." Allie held up her badge. "Detective Krenshaw. I just got off the phone with him ten minutes ago."

"Oh, right, Detective. Um, please sit down and I'll let him know you're here." She motioned back to one of three cushioned chairs along the wall.

"He has one minute. I'm timing it." Allie looked at her watch and leaned against the wall, having no intention of sitting down. The second hand ticked past the seven.

The secretary forced a smile. "One moment, Detective." She ducked her head and went to the double doors that led to the inner office where the mayor would be.

Allie watched the second hand tick by. He was taking too long to invite her in. She didn't like it. She should have been welcomed immediately. He of all people should know what had happened today.

Just as the second hand ticked past the five, the double doors opened again and the secretary stepped out. "Detective Krenshaw, he's ready for you."

"It's about time." Allie stepped into the office and the double doors were closed behind her.

"Detective Krenshaw. Good to see you're back on duty." The mayor greeted and motioned to one of the chairs in front of his desk.

Why did these people keep trying to get her to sit down? There was no time to sit. They needed to act! "Mayor Norton, I have no time for pleasantries. You know why I'm here."

"Yes, you mentioned on the phone about some files of mine being found at a crime scene. What files were found?"

"Financials. All of your benefactors. Since you know that, you must also know that one of my partners was stabbed and robbed of those files." Allie stared at him, waiting to gauge his reaction.

Dan averted his eyes, looking down at his desk. "I'm sorry for that, Detective."

He was sincere. Allie nodded. "Thank you, but I need to find who did it. You know who took those files."

His head snapped up, his eyes locking with hers. "I do?" He asked, pointing at his chest.

"Yes, you do."

"Am I being interrogated here, Detective?"

"Yes. Don't you think I deserve some answers? Ever since that file was found, two of my partners have been hurt." Her voice wavered slightly, her thoughts going to Marcus in the ICU. Though the doctor's said they were hopeful, she knew better. No one would make eye contact with her. Marcus was dying and someone would answer for that.

"You have *no* right to come into *my* office and take that attitude with me. I could have you fired on the spot!"

"But you won't because you want to know where those files are just as much as I do. You've hired people to do your dirty work before. You know whose work this is." Allie slapped his desk with both hands, leaning close. "Now tell me who you hired to get those files back."

Dan took a deep breath and sat back in his chair, crossing his legs and resting his folded hands in his lap. "How dare you."

"Answer the question, Dan. I want this guy."

"I didn't hire anyone." Dan shook his head. "I wasn't even aware of the missing files until you called me. And now you tell me that you don't even have them and they're out there floating around for

112

the world to see." He stood up and pressed his knuckles into the desk as he leaned forward, his face inches from hers. His eyes locked with hers and he lowered his voice. "I suggest you do your *job*. I'm not doing it for you." He straightened and smoothed his clothes, clearing his throat. "You may see yourself out, Detective Krenshaw."

Jaw clenched, she spun on her heel and moved to the door. She stopped with her hand on the knob and turned back around to face him. "I *will* find him and if this all leads back to you, you'll be sorry."

"Are you threatening me?"

"No, promising you." Allie pursed her lips and jerked the door open. The mayor's secretary stood up when she came out. Allie didn't acknowledge her but marched right out of the office and back out into the streets. Tears threatened at the back of her throat. She sucked her breath in through her teeth and let out a low growl, her fists clenched at her sides. "One more reason to hate politicians."

*****

Allie snatched her phone off the cradle when the ringing filled the empty precinct. "Krenshaw."

"You sound mad." Marcus' raspy voice sounded like music to her ears.

"You're awake! Why are you calling me? You should be resting. You just got blown up."

"Nah, the doctors don't know what they're talking about. They tried to keep me from calling, even took my phone away."

Allie frowned. "Then how are you calling me now?"

He went into a fit of coughing and groaned. "Megan came down to visit. She's had contraband on her this whole time and no one has noticed." He chuckled lightly before going into another fit of coughing.

"Megan should be in bed too." Allie sighed. "I'll come down and see you."

"Visiting hours are over."

"I'll scale the wall if I have to. I'm coming to see you. We have a case to work. You think the explosion lets you off the hook? I don't think so. Walk it off, Marcus." Allie started gathering up her files to take to the hospital with her.

"What if I'm tired?"

"You'll get over it. I'll bring Chinese."

Marcus sighed. "Fine, I'll stay up."

"Does Megan want anything?" Allie heard Marcus' muffled voice talking to Megan. She pulled open the top drawer of her desk and dug three dollars from her change jar to get sodas at the vending machine.

"She said she wants sweet and sour chicken and pork fried rice."

"Both?"

"Yes, both. Don't be hatin' on Megan."

Allie scoffed. "Right, I wouldn't. I'm hanging up. I'll be there in twenty minutes." Allie hung up the receiver and picked up her stack of files. She hurried to the elevator and pushed the down button. While she waited, she pulled out her phone and called in their order so it would be ready when she got there. She was anxious to see Marcus.

She never expected him to wake up but she was glad he had.

*****

Marcus did his best to mask his pain but didn't feel he was pulling it off. Allie had gotten to the hospital shortly after he called her. She was an emotional mess. His accident had been two days ago. He doubted she got a wink of sleep in that time. She'd invaded his dreams. Ever since he got her back from Bastian, he'd been more aware of his feelings. Now that he'd had a near death experience, he was ready to put an end to this friendship. He wanted more.

Allie chewed the end of her pen as she read a file. Did she know how crazy he was about her? Did she want more? What if he asked her for more and it ruined everything they had? What if it didn't? He was willing to take the chance."

"Megan fell asleep." He mentioned and glanced over at the young woman slouched down in her chair. "She's healing up well."

Allie nodded. "She's being released tomorrow. I think Megan's been nagging them but they wanted to be sure before they let her leave." Allie smiled at him. "Sound familiar?"

Marcus smiled and lay head back on the pillow. "She's a lot like you. I noticed that." He turned his head to face her. "Did you call my sister?"

"Yeah, I left a message for her to call me and she didn't get back with me until yesterday because she was at work or something. She left after I talked to her so she should be here in the morning,

I think. I told her not to be stupid and drive straight through. It's an eighteen hour drive and that's too much for her to do on her own. She's been calling around meal times to check on you."

Marcus sighed. "She's going to be mad at me for this." Marcus stared up at the white, square ceiling tiles. He frowned at a light red dot on one of the tiles. Wincing, he looked back over at Allie. "So I'm guessing you went and talked to Mayor Norton."

"Yeah, a lot of good that did. He basically told me to go do my job and catch this guy and to stop bothering him."

He could imagine how that conversation went. Allie would have been mad and the mayor would have been on the defense. She didn't always have the best people skills. They were worse when she was upset. Someday he'd teach her how to communicate respectfully with people to get what she wanted. It would be awhile. She was the worst student.

"Do you remember anything before the explosion?"

Marcus shook his head. "Not really. I remember talking to the mayor's secretary on the phone."

"You mean flirting with her? I saw her. She's your type."

"My type?" He looked over at her, somewhat amused. "And what is my type, Al?"

Allie rolled her eyes. "Tall and thin. You like long hair that's curly and typically brunette. You've never gone for blondes. Oh, and you've always leaned toward brown eyes."

"Cuz it reminds me of chocolate. I like chocolate." He winked and waited for another eye roll from her. He wasn't disappointed. He chuckled. "I wasn't flirting with her, for your information. I happen to know she's married. Her husband goes to my gym."

"You go to the gym?"

"You think I look this good naturally?" Marcus looked over at her and waited for the next eye roll. "You should stop doing that. One of these times, your eyes are going to get stuck like that."

"Okay, Dad." She mocked and stuck her tongue out.

"I wouldn't want that in my mouth either." He wanted to laugh at his own humor but knew it would only send him into a fit of coughing so he suppressed it.

"Well, I can tell you're feeling better." Allie said dryly and shook her head. "I don't know why I even bothered coming. You're such a pain."

"You love it." Marcus looked down at the file in his hands. "Did you talk to Kent Bradley?"

"No. I stopped by his office but he is supposedly out of town." Allie scoffed. "This is election prime time and he is out of town. I find that hard to believe. I think he's just avoiding me. Why would he leave town when he is behind in the polls? Shouldn't he be *in* town working to get more votes? I mean, that's what I would be doing."

"You gonna run for mayor now?"

"Ha! I don't think so. Too much headache if you ask me." Allie handed him another file. "This is everything I learned from Jenna's apartment. I updated your file to add in the posters we found and the dart board."

"The dartboard?" Marcus scanned the file until he found the dartboard. He raised his eyebrows. "Well, that's different. Did you ask Dan if he knew Jenna?"

Allie winced. "No, I was kinda mad. I don't think he'll want to talk to me."

"I can talk to him."

"Marcus, you can't even walk. How are you going to go talk to him?"

"His secretary is my type, remember?" He winked and laughed when Allie buried her face in her hands and groaned. "I'm kidding. I'll ask him to come by. He'll come because it will be good press for him to visit an officer that was nearly killed in the line of duty. You just have to know how to work these politicians. It's easier than you think."

"Or maybe I'll just leave talking to politicians up to you. I hate having to talk to them."

"I know you do." Marcus closed the files. "I'll call him tomorrow. However, if Maddie is going to be here in the morning, I really need to get some sleep. I'm sure she's going to be an emotional mess."

"True. I'll let you get some sleep. I'll stop by mid-morning so you have some time alone with Maddie. Does she have a key to your apartment or does she need to stay at my house?"

Marcus met Allie's eyes. "Do you need her to stay at your house?"

Allie hesitated. "No, it's okay."

"Have you slept since my accident?"

Allie pursed her lips, telling him everything he needed to know.

"I'll tell Maddie to stay at your house. It will probably be better that she's not alone. She tends to think too much and jump to conclusions." Marcus reached for Allie's hand. "Thanks for taking care of everything."

"It's the least I could do. I'm the one that should be in that bed." Allie leaned in and pressed a kiss to his cheek. "I'm glad you're okay." She whispered in his ear. She pulled back and met his eyes. "Don't scare me like that again."

His heart fluttered in his chest. "I'll try my best." He croaked and cleared his throat, releasing her hand.

Allie went over and gently shook Megan's shoulder. Megan woke up and trudged from the room. Her eyes met his. "Get some rest."

"I will. I still have Megan's phone so text me when you get home. If you need to, call."

"Okay. Good night, Marcus." Allie raised her hand in a wave before disappearing down the hallway.

Marcus rested his head back and stared at the ceiling. There was no doubt in his mind now. He wanted more and he'd risk anything to get it. Marcus stared at Megan's phone, waiting for Allie's call.

9

Allie flipped through the pictures of Jenna's apartment. It was odd someone would want to kill this girl. She was a college student who was just trying to figure out who she was. Allie remembered those days. You tried on all different sorts of personalities and job ideas to see which one fit you best. Because of her age, switching from one political party to the other wasn't a complete shock. Stealing files, however, was.

She flipped her wrist over and glanced at her watch. Ten minutes until her meeting with Kent Bradley. She gathered up the pictures and straightened them in a pile. The corner of one caught on the others and she pulled it out and put it at the front. She stopped a moment and stared at the picture of Jenna's closet.

She'd been so distracted by the dartboard, she missed the stack of campaign signs. Allie held the picture close to her face, examining the signs. They were pieces of cardboard on top of metal frames. Her mouth dropped and she lowered the pictures to her desk. How could she have missed that? This connected all of the cases they were working on.

Someone was killing people who were supporting Dan Norton.

Allie shoved the pictures and files in a messenger bag. Flipping the bag over her shoulder, she hurried to the elevator. She hit the button several times even though she knew it wouldn't make the elevator understand her rush. She glanced up at the numbers as they flashed the location of the elevator. She didn't have time for this.

Allie darted toward the stairs. She fumbled down the three flights of stairs to the parking garage. She jerked open the door of Marcus' car and the engine roared to life. Flipping on the lights and sirens, she sped to Dan Norton's office. Naturally, if someone was killing the people voting for him, their next stop would be to his office to kill him. Allie just hoped she wasn't too late.

*****

He'd been sloppy on the last two jobs. He was man enough to admit when he'd made a mistake. It was an easy fix, though. One shot and all of his problems would be over. Tony twisted the pieces of his gun together and snapped the scope on top.

He took a long drink of his water before raising himself up on his knees to peek over the edge of the building. He aimed his gun at the office window and peered through scope. Where was she? He checked the office one floor up but she wasn't there. Frowning, he pointed the gun in the air and squinted to make sure he was looking in the right place.

A glint caught his eye and then he spotted her. The corner of his mouth hitched up in a smile. "Gotcha." He aimed his gun, her head in his crosshairs. He put his finger on the trigger, checked his wind speed and…

A shot echoed through the streets below.

Tony watched as the glass window in front of his target shattered. She fell back into the room. Tony took shelter behind the top of the building, his gun aiming toward the buildings around him. He hadn't fired that shot. There was another shooter on one of the rooftops.

Another shot sounded and a bullet pierced the wall next to his head. A man dressed in all black stepped out from behind a generator, his sniper rifle aimed at Tony. The man took a few slow steps forward, his aim steady on Tony's head.

"What do you want?" Tony demanded.

"Stay away from her."

"What's it to you?"

The man closed the distance between them with a few quick steps. He knelt down, his gun mere inches from Tony's forehead. "I'm a friend. Keep away from her or next time, I won't miss putting a bullet between your eyes."

Tony stared at the man in the mask. His light blue eyes were steady and calm. This man was a professional. It wouldn't help his cause to get on this guy's bad side. "Fine. I'll leave her alone; just keep her out of my business."

"And what business is that?"

"*My* business ain't any of *your* business."

His blue eyes rolled upward. "Whatever."

He took a piece of paper from his pocket, rolled it up and pushed it down into the barrel of his gun. He tossed the gun to the side and walked away, pulling his mask off as he went. He never turned around and Tony never got a good look at his face before he jumped off the side of the building.

Sirens sounded loud and clear. He had to get inside before the cops got here. Scrambling to his feet, he grabbed the bag he kept his gun in and hurried to the stair door. Fumbling down the stairs, he rushed to apartment 32 and let himself in. He went directly to the bedroom and stashed his gun between the bed spring and mattress. He could take it apart later. Right now, he had to work on an alibi.

*****

Marcus groaned, the skin on his side stretching and burning as he slipped into his shirt. He wasn't about to argue with the doctor who saw fit to release him, but part of him wondered if he was ready.

A knock sounded on the door before Maddie's head popped around the corner. She smiled when she saw him. "You look a lot better. I knew my coming would heal you."

"Oh, is that all it took?" Marcus managed a shaky smile despite the burning pains in his arms and chest.

Maddie rested her hand lightly on his shoulder. "The doctor said you could go home, but not back to work so we are going back to your apartment and you are going to rest."

Even if he wanted to, he couldn't argue with her about resting. His body was already begging to go back to bed. "That's fine, but we're going to Allie's house, not my apartment."

Maddie frowned and shook her head. "No, you only want to go there to keep close to the case. That's not happening. I'll call Mom if I have to."

Marcus took a deep breath, preparing himself for the pain he knew he'd feel putting on his shoes. Try as he might to not make a sound, a pained gasp escaped his lips. "Sorry, I'm fine." He assured quickly but that didn't stop her from picking up his shoes and putting them on for him.

As the pain subsided he explained. "I'm going to Allie's because she needs me. It's not for the case, it's for other reasons."

Maddie stopped all movement and looked up at him, her eyes alit with mischief. "Did you finally man up and tell her you loved her? Are you guys dating?"

"You wish." Marcus shook his head. "Since her abduction, she hasn't been doing well. She's had terrible nightmares and she doesn't like to be alone. I'm just helping her out."

Maddie rolled her eyes. "I swear, don't you ever get tired of being the good ol boy? You need to tell that woman how you feel or she's just going to keep seeing you as a friend and you'll never get what you really want." Maddie jerked on his shoe laces, tightening the shoe too tight around his foot.

"Watch it there!" Marcus jerked his foot away and rolled his ankle to help loosen the shoe. "I'm going to talk to her, eventually. She's been through a traumatic experience. It's not exactly the best time to talk about all of this."

Maddie pulled his foot back over and continued tying his shoe. "You're wrong. It's the *perfect* time to talk about all of this."

"Whatever. I'm not going to argue with you about this. I *am* going to stay at Allie's."

"Fine. I'll get your bag." Maddie ducked into the bathroom and came out with the overnight bag she'd brought him the night before. "I'm staying there with you, though."

Marcus smiled. "You're worried about me." He teased and dropped his arm around her shoulders, pulling her close. "I'm touched."

Maddie laughed. "Whatever. You're just a big baby and I know you'll want someone close by to take care of you."

They headed for the door. "Does that mean you'll massage my feet tonight?"

"Ew! No! Your feet stink!"

Marcus laughed and checked his phone. He had four missed calls from Allie. Marcus dialed her number despite Maddie's protests. When Allie answered, he knew something was wrong. As soon as he heard the words, he didn't want to believe it. "Are you sure?"

"Yeah, I don't know what to do." Allie said in a hoarse whisper.

Marcus glanced at Maddie's disapproving and shook his head. "Stay put. I'll be there in ten minutes."

"Marcus…"

"Take me to the mayor's office, now." He moved as fast as his body would let him to Maddie's car and slid into the front seat.

"This is ridiculous." Maddie said as she pulled out onto the road. "You just got blown up three days ago. What could possibly be so important that they need you there?"

"The mayor's been shot."

*****

Allie stood out front of city hall waiting for Marcus. If she had any doubts that Nate Harris was still out there, they were now gone. She fingered the bandage on her upper arm. It was still a bit hard to believe that he'd actually shot her.

When CSU had found the note in the gun she hadn't wanted to believe it, but it was just his style. He was the old school, creative, message in a bottle type guy. Allie looked at the note once more, lifted it to her nose and breathed in the smell of gun powder and Nate's cologne. The note had definitely been from him and he proved he was the shooter by putting it in the gun he'd used to fire the shot.

Marcus would not be happy.

An old red Camry pulled up to the curb and Marcus struggled to lift himself out of the car.

Allie hurried over to him, not missing the worried look on his face when he saw her arm. "You're hurt."

"I'm fine. It's just a graze." Allie handed him the note. His fingers closed around the note, but she didn't release it until he met her eyes. "Don't blow this out of proportion but I thought you should know. No more secrets." Allie watched his face as he read the note. He was angry.

"It isn't signed. How do you know it's Nate?"

Allie bit her lip and shrugged. "It smells like him and the handwriting is his."

Marcus lifted the paper to his nose and rolled his eyes. "Of course. He's like a love-sick teenager." He limped up the steps on his way to the mayor's office. Allie followed after him. "How's the mayor?"

"Still in shock but the bullet barely grazed him. I got the brunt of it."

"And from this note, you were the target." Marcus stopped and turned to face her. "I *will* catch him, Allie. I know you still think he's this good guy, but he's not. He just *shot* you."

Allie pursed her lips. "I know he isn't a good guy. I'm just telling you that he is being forced to do these things! And his note says if he hadn't taken the shot, someone else would have. That other person probably wouldn't have just shot me, they probably would have killed me."

"Oh, so shooting people is how you show your love now? I guess I missed the memo!" Pain radiated in his eyes. She wasn't sure if it was physical or emotional pain. He'd always had a hard time dealing with her relationship with Nate but she still didn't know why.

Allie sighed and watched him limp into the building. Maddie came up and stopped next to her. Allie met her look. "Did the doctor give him any pain pills?"

"Yeah, but we haven't filled the prescription yet. Who is this guy?"

"Nate Harris."

"Ah." Maddie nodded and forced a smile. "Three piece suit guy."

Allie chuckled. "Yeah, that's him. Marcus told you about him?"

"Oh, mostly just complained about him."

Allie turned to Maddie and crossed her arms. "Did he tell you why he hates Nate so much?"

"You mean, besides the fact that he just shot you?" Maddie shook her head. "I know, but I'm not going to tell you. That's something you have to figure out for yourself." Maddie turned and started down the steps to her car. "Let Marcus know I went to pick up his medicine and I'll be back." She called over her shoulder and was gone a minute later.

Allie took the steps two at a time to catch up to Marcus. Something was going on here and she needed some answers. Marcus couldn't just be thankful that Nate had possibly saved her life.

This would have been the second attempt on her life. That meant she was getting close to solving this case and it really did have something to do with the upcoming mayoral election. Dan Norton had won the primary election. The secondary election would take place in two weeks. She had two weeks to hunt this killer down or the next bullet fired might not be for her but Mayor Norton.

10

Allie looked over at Marcus. He had hardly spoken to her since yesterday. She'd been surprised he had stayed at his apartment instead of at her house like planned. It was clear he was upset, but it was unclear as to why he was so upset. If he decided to act so hurt by all of this, then that was fine with her. At least he was going through the motions of doing his job.

"Are you sure you're up for this interview? I don't mind doing it by myself."

Marcus put the car in park and unbuckled his seatbelt. "I'm good."

Allie noted the campaign sign for Kent Bradley in the front yard. It was amazing that to stay safe you had to have that sign in your yard. As they headed to the front door, Allie slowed her walk. "What are you going to say to them?"

"We just need to play this cool." Marcus rapped on the door. "We've done this a thousand times, Allie."

"Are you gonna ask them about Megan?"

"No, leave Megan out of this."

Allie nodded, biting the inside of her cheek. She didn't want to leave Megan out of it. The girl had been stabbed and robbed of information on Kent Bradley's rival. If Kent refused to cooperate and act like he knew nothing about it, she'd force him to admit it.

The door opened and Cara Bradley answered the door. She was dressed to the nines in her long burgundy evening dress that glittered in the sunlight. Her long blonde curls were bundled on top of her head to give everyone a view of her shimmering diamond necklace.

"Can I help you?" Cara asked as she looked Marcus up and down, biting her lower lip.

"I'm Detective Marcus, this is Detective Krenshaw." Marcus flashed his badge. "We're looking for your husband, is he at home?"

Cara frowned and shook her head. "No, he left for the office about ten minutes ago. What is all of this about?"

"We just needed to ask him a few questions. We'll see if we can't find him at the office. Thank you." Marcus' eyes locked with hers. He didn't trust Cara Bradley. As the headed to the car, he stayed silent, even opened the door for her. He glanced around as she got in the car. "We need to have someone watch this house."

"I agree. I'll call Megan."

"Really? Don't you think she should be resting?" Marcus closed the door and walked around the car. He slowly got behind the wheel and sighed.

"Shouldn't *you* be resting? She's been recuperating longer than you have. I'm texting her. This will at least give her something to do. She can sit and watch, if he leaves, she can follow him. No big deal."

"Ashton won't like it."

"What Ashton doesn't know won't hurt him." Allie pulled out her phone and sent the text. "Are we going to his office or are we just going to sit here?"

"I thought we'd just sit here for a while." Marcus said dryly and started up the car. "How's your arm?"

"Fine." Allie reached up and covered her arm with her hand. Once more she wondered if she should track Nate down. If he knew someone was gunning for her, then he also had to know who it was. Maybe it was time to get him out of his shell. Only one person knew more about Nate than she did. "Will you take me to the prison?"

"Why?" Marcus frowned at her before pulling out onto the road.

"I think we can both agree that we need to find Nate, right?"

"Yes, and put him behind bars where he belongs."

"And who is the one person who knows who Nate is?"

Marcus shook his head. "We don't know that for sure. He could be bluffing."

"Only one way to find out." Allie shrugged. "You know he'll talk to me."

"I don't think this is smart, Allie. You're still having nightmares about him. Besides, I don't think he knows as much as he would lead you to believe."

Allie glanced up at Marcus, narrowing his eyes. He knew something she didn't. Had he already talked to Bastian at the prison? "What are you keeping from me, Marcus?"

"Nothing." He answered quickly.

Allie scoffed and shook her head. "I don't believe this. How long, Marcus? How long have you been visiting him?"

Marcus sighed and ran his hand through his hair. "I haven't been visiting him. Not really."

"Will you just stop lying to me?" She demanded and crossed her arms over her chest, her eyes staring out the window but seeing nothing. "We agreed. No more secrets."

"Yes, yes we agreed that, but this is different, Allie. I was just trying to protect you."

Her head snapped around. "To *protect* me? Protect me from what, Marcus? Certainly not from Bastian. The man would never hurt me!"

"From yourself!" His voice raised, his eyes piercing her heart. "You haven't been the same since you got back." He glanced back at the road, his hands loosened their grip on the steering wheel and his shoulders dropped. "He's done something to you, even if you don't realize it. It's his name you cry out in your nightmares. You scream for him to stop. You keep saying no." He slowed the car and came to a stop at a red light. His eyes met hers and he reached over and rested his hand on her arm. "You're not the only one who is scared by your nightmares, Allie. I'm living them too."

Allie swallowed hard and pulled away from him. "You still should have told me." Her voice cracked slightly. She looked back out the window. Was Marcus right? Was it better for her to stay away? Maybe visiting Bastian in prison would be a good thing. Seeing him one last time, knowing that he couldn't get to her and she was safe. Maybe her nightmares would stop.

For the first time Allie wondered if maybe she should go talk to the psychiatrist again. He might be able to help her with this. Marcus was right. Bastian had done something to her. He hadn't harmed her in any way physically, but mentally and emotionally he'd torn her apart and now she wasn't the only one suffering. She'd never thought about Marcus having to listen to her having nightmares. Was she selfish for not seeing it or was it just the result of trauma?

Either way, she still wanted to go visit Bastian and she told Marcus as much.

Marcus sighed, propping his elbow up on the car door and resting his chin in his hand. "You really think it'll help?"

Allie shrugged, rubbing her hands on her pants. "Only one way to find out."

"Fine. I'll take you out there." Marcus flipped on his blinker to turn the car around. "I don't want you in the room with him. We can put him in an interrogation room where you can watch from behind a mirror. I'll ask him the questions, you watch him for signs of lying."

"I could get information from him if he could see me."

"You'll wait behind the glass. If after seeing him again, you want to come in the room, knock on the glass. Until then, I refuse to let him have the satisfaction of seeing you again."

"He's been asking for me?"

"Every day."

*****

Marcus stood in the back room with Allie, watching her as she watched Bastian being escorted into the room. Her eyes were locked on the man who had held her captive for ten days. Her hands gripped the edge of the table she was leaning back against. She seemed to be holding herself together rather well.

As soon as Bastian was cuffed to the table, Marcus knew it was his time to go in. "Remember what I said. If you want to come in, if you think he can handle it, just knock on the glass three times and I'll say yes or no. The guard will let you in."

Allie's head jerked up and down twice. "And if he's lying I knock once."

"Yes. You know this guy better than any of us. I know you can do this, but I want *you* to know that you don't have to."

Allie looked up at him for the first time since they arrived at the prison. "I can do this. I'll be fine." Allie looked back at Bastian. "He's our best shot at finding Nate and putting an end to these murders."

Marcus nodded and left the room. He hated talking to Bastian. Every time he saw that smug smile he wanted to scratch his face off. Women were writing to Bastian in jail, falling in love with the manipulative pig. Part of him wondered if Allie had fallen under his charms.

"Welcome back, Detective Marcus." Bastian smiled, spreading his hands open on the table. "I would stand, but that's quite impossible."

"That's good." Marcus nodded to the guard and he left Marcus alone with Bastian. "I'm here to ask you a few questions about the two people you abducted."

A soft smile graced his features. "You mean, Allie? Come on, say her name." He laughed under his breath and sat back in his chair. "It's killing you isn't it? That I got her and you didn't. You've loved her for two years and she hasn't given you a second glance. I spend mere days with her and win her affection."

A single knock sounded on the glass behind him and his conscious would put at ease. "We're not here to talk about her. We're here to talk about Nate Harris."

Bastian scoffed and leaned forward. "You guys haven't even figured out his real name yet? You're pathetic." He spat out and glanced at the walls around him.

"His real name? You know it?"

"Of course I do." Bastian sat back in his chair, one corner of his mouth lifted up in a smile.

A single knock sounded on the glass behind him. Marcus cleared his throat and met Bastian's eyes. "Tell me what you think his real name is."

Bastian looked from Marcus to the glass behind him and back. "Who's behind that glass?" His face softened and he sat up straighter, scooting his chair in. "Is Allie back there?"

"What makes you think someone is back there? You know I always come alone."

"Someone keeps knocking on the glass."

"It's probably faulty pipes." Marcus folded his hands on the table in front of him. "Now, back to my question. What do you think Nate's real name is?"

"I don't *think* I know what his real name is, I know." Bastian glanced back at the glass. "I know she's back there. I know you're keeping her from me." Bastian's eyes met his. "No name until I see her."

"All right, I don't need the name. Do you know where Nate lives or where he lived when you knew him? I assume you followed him and knew everything about him as you probably do me and anyone else in my partner's life."

Bastian's jaw clenched. "Allie. Just say her name." He demanded and his hands clenched in fists. "Allie is a beautiful name, though not her real name. Her real name is Alicia but she just shortened it to Allie because that's what her dad always called her." Bastian cocked his head to the side and looked quizzically at Marcus. "She really misses her dad."

"We aren't here to talk about my partner. We're here to talk about Nate. If you can't stick to the topic then I'll just leave and find my answers elsewhere."

"A name for a name. A place for a place."

Marcus sighed and cleared his throat. "All right. What name do you want?"

Bastian laughed humorlessly. When his eyes met Marcus' they were stone cold. "Your name. I want your name."

Marcus frowned. "My name? You already know my name."

"Your first name. No one knows it and I was never able to find it. I'm sure Allie would be happy to hear your name as well."

"She already knows it." Marcus shrugged. "I was in the hospital. I'm sure she saw it on my chart." A knock sounded on the glass behind him and he had to smile. "If knowing my name will get me Nate's real name, fine. But this isn't going to be a simple exchange. You will give me his last name, I'll give you my first, and then you give me his first name. Deal?"

Bastian raised his eyebrows, the corners of his mouth turning down as he considered the offer. "Deal. His last name is Smith." Bastian smiled and leaned forward. "Your turn, Detective."

Three knocks sounded on the glass behind him. Marcus shook his head. "No."

Bastian slammed his fist into the table. "We had a deal!"

Marcus stood up. "I'll be right back." He left the room despite Bastian's loud complaints and went back to see Allie. "You're not going in there. He'll tear you apart."

"It's not that. I wanted you to come. I think he's lying. How can we know for sure he's giving us the right name? I mean, come on, Smith? That's the best he could come up with?"

Marcus chuckled. "Well, that's what I thought, but then again, if you were going to make up a name, why make up Smith? Bastian is smarter than that. He isn't your average criminal, you know?" Marcus smiled at her as he leaned against the wall and crossed his arms over his chest. "So it's not true?"

"What's not true?"

"You didn't look at my medical chart to see what my name was?"

Allie bit her lip, forcing the corners of her mouth down. "Why would I care?"

"Ha! Oh, I don't know, maybe because you've been nagging me for the past two years to admit my real name? Come on, you didn't look? You weren't even tempted?"

Allie smiled and shook her head. "You need to go back in there and finish questioning him. If you really want to reveal your name, be my guest."

"I'm not ashamed." Marcus opened the door and stopped, glancing back at her. "Actually, I am ashamed, just not of you knowing it." When she looked at him, he winked and went back to the room with Bastian. "Sorry about that. Where were we?"

Bastian started grinding his teeth. "Your name, Detective. You'd better hold up your end of the deal."

"I have every intention to." He glanced at the mirror behind him before looking back at Bastian. "You said his last name was Smith?" Marcus pulled out his phone and typed it in. He locked his phone, set it down and folded his hands on the table in front of him. "I'm not lying to you. The name I am about to reveal is indeed my birth name that my mother gave me and no matter what you think, you still need to uphold your end of this deal and reveal Mr. Smith's first name."

"This is absurd. You're stalling! Just tell me the name!"

"Handsome." Marcus cleared his throat and stared at his interlocked fingers.

"Excuse me?"

Marcus cleared his throat again and shifted in his chair. "It's Handsome."

"Handsome Marcus? You expect me to believe your name is Handsome Marcus?" Bastian scoffed and sat back shaking his head. "Does your family have a history of mental disorders or is it just your mother?"

Marcus shook his head. "Come on, I told you my first name. What is Mr. Smith's first name?"

Bastian shook his head. "I'm not saying. You're lying to me."

"I'm not." Marcus reached into his wallet and pulled out his driver's license. He held it up for Bastian to read. "There it is."

"You could have made that."

"Why would I?"

"To trick me."

"I have nothing left to hide, Bastian. Now, we had a deal. What's his first name?"

Bastian shook his head. "I'll only tell Allie. I know she's here."

Marcus sighed and stood up. "I guess we're at a loss then. My partner isn't coming in here." Just as he said the words, the door to the interrogation room opened and Allie walked in, the door locking behind her.

"Give me the name, Bastian."

His entire demeanor softened. It's like he became a new person the moment she walked in the room. A smile graced his features. "I've missed you."

Allie looked up at Marcus and nodded once before sitting down in the chair he held for her.

"I'm not here to chat, Bastian. I need Nate's real name and I need it now."

"Do you miss me at all?"

"Answer the question, Bastian." Marcus grabbed a chair from a back corner and set it down next to Allie. "We aren't here to play games. Lives are at stake."

Bastian sighed and seemed almost shy as he stared at his twiddling thumbs. "I can give you the name." The corners of his mouth turned upward. "For a kiss."

"I'm not kissing you, Bastian." Marcus said and rested his hand on Allie's shoulder. "You said you'd give Allie the name, now do it."

Bastian glared at him. "Of course I don't want a kiss from you!" He bellowed. His features softened as he looked at Allie. "If you would, my love, it would make my life worth living again." He tried to reach for her hands, but the handcuffs prevented him.

"Fine. Give me the name first."

Marcus stared at Allie in surprise. "No, Allie, I won't let you do this."

"It's my choice Marcus."

"It's nothing we haven't done before." Bastian sneered.

Marcus gritted his teeth. "Just because it was done before under duress doesn't mean it has to happen again." He turned his attention to Allie. "Don't do this."

"The name, Bastian."

"Shawn. That's S-H-A-W-N, not S-E-A-N. Shawn Smith." He wiggled his eyebrows at Marcus and leaned toward Allie. "How about that kiss?"

Allie stood up and set her hand down on the table in front of Bastian. When she picked it up there was a piece of silver-wrapped chocolate on the table in front of him. "This one will last longer." Allie looked at Marcus. "Let's go."

11

8 days to Election Day

He was so cocky. Did he really think he could be protected by three police officers who couldn't even protect themselves? I guess it was part of his job to trust the justice system. Tony clenched his teeth, forcing a smile as Al stepped from the podium and walked toward him.

As soon as he saw Tony, Al's smile dissolved into a scowl. "What are you doing here?"

"I came to see how things were going. Can't I stop by and check on you? We were friends once upon a time."

Al scoffed. "I haven't seen you for two years and now all of a sudden you want to be friends again? I don't think so, Anthony. You need to leave before someone sees you. The last thing I need is another seeded scandal on my hands because you did something you weren't supposed to do. The election is in the bag."

"How do you know that?"

Al rolled his eyes. "I've been doing this a long time, Anthony. I know what it takes to win and I'm not afraid to do it."

"Yes, too bad your loyal fans are all dying. Tell me; were you the father of Jenna's baby?"

Al's head whipped around, his eyes narrowing. "Who told you about that?"

"Ha! Who do you think?" Tony rolled his eyes. "You're really not as smart as you think you are, Al. I've got so much dirt on you it would ruin your whole campaign."

Al's hands clenched at his sides. "What do you want, Anthony?"

"I want to come to Sunday dinner." Surely Al wouldn't turn him away. What was one dinner? He hadn't been invited to a Sunday dinner for weeks. He might even be willing to sit through a church service if it meant he could attend.

"Out of the question. You're not getting anywhere near my family." Al took a deep breath. "Do you have a second demand I might be able to meet?"

Tony grabbed Al by the front of the shirt and slammed him against the wall. "One dinner, Al, that's all it would have taken, but you've left me no choice." Tony pulled him close, his eyes glaring into Al's as he whispered his threats. "You will rue the day you rejected me." He threw the man back against the wall and marched away.

As he stepped out into the sunlight, he glanced down at the strand of hair pinched between his fingers. A small smile teased the corners of his mouth. Dan Norton had enjoyed his last day in the sun. It was time for the rains to come down and the flood waters to come up and demolish everything he once held dear.

*****

Allie glanced at Marcus still asleep on the couch and tiptoed to the front door. She turned the locks, hoping the chain scraping and two lock clicks wouldn't wake him. She turned the knob and gave the door one firm jerk. It opened with minimal scraping. Marcus sighed and twisted around on the couch before settling back down to sleep.

Biting her lip, she stepped out onto the porch and pulled the door shut behind her. She pulled out Marcus' car keys and went to his car. Not for the first time did she wish she still had her car. She'd loved it. Maybe she should start shopping around for a new car. She wasn't sure her insurance would help her with an explosion claim.

As soon as she was settled behind the wheel, her phone rang. Groaning, she glanced at the caller id and saw it was Captain Ashton calling. Allie cleared her throat and answered. "Krenshaw."

"I've got another one for you and Marcus. Body is cold. Accident happened a few days ago but it was ruled a homicide."

"Who is the victim? What happened?"

"Car accident. Name is Evan Albright. It appears someone disabled the brakes. As soon as he got on the highway, he didn't stand a chance. The accident turned into that big thirteen car pile-up."

Allie shook her head. "How many others were killed?"

"Three, but we think they were just collateral damage and Evan was the actual target."

Allie nodded. "Any connection to our current cases?"

"That's your job, Allie. The car is available and Dana has Mr. Albright's body. His wife will be in today to identify the body and I've already informed her we need to ask her a few questions."

"Right. I'll let Megan and Marcus know."

"Megan is here, she already knows."

Allie frowned. "I thought she was following Kent Bradley."

"Kent Bradley is here and he's not very happy that you and Marcus spoke to his wife."

Allie smiled. "Good. I have to run a personal errand this morning and Marcus is still asleep. I'll be in later today. Let me know what you learn." Allie hung up and turned the engine over. She pulled out of the driveway and headed downtown. She parked in the old parking garage next to the white industrial building. It was an old run-down building that had been here for as long as she could remember. She used to love it. It was one of many landmarks she had.

Emerging from the car, she took a deep breath and went into the building. She took the elevator up to the sixth floor, commonly referred to as the number of the devil. She couldn't think of anything more fitting. The doors opened and she proceeded down the hallway to the last door on the left. With one deep breath she rapped on the door three times.

"Come in."

Allie twisted the knob and stepped into Dr. Seaver's office.

"Allie, have a seat. Coffee?"

She shook her head and sat down in one of the overstuffed chairs. She squirmed in her chair, wishing she hadn't come. He took his time pouring the coffee before he sat down in his chair and nodded. "It happened." She blurted out. Her eyes stung with unshed tears. Her throat was on fire. She took a shaky breath. "You were right. I saw him and I could barely keep it together." A tear cascaded down her cheek. "And Marcus was there."

Dr. Seaver nodded. "Where did you see him? Why?"

"For a case. He had information. He knew things and I needed what he had." Allie shrugged and sniffed. "I thought it was the logical thing to do and Marcus tried to talk me out of it, but I was stubborn and said no."

"What happened at this meeting?"

Allie sighed, squeezing her hands together. "Nothing at first. I was in another room just watching behind the glass." She swallowed past the lump in her throat, the action making the burning all the worse. "He knew I was there. He kept looking at the glass and every time he did, we made eye contact." She folded her arms around her middle, feeling cold.

"Then what happened, Allie."

She took a deep breath. "Marcus just questioned him until finally he said he would only give me the name."

"So you went in the room."

Allie nodded. "Marcus said no, he refused, but again, I was stupid and just did things my own way." Her trembling hand went to cover her quivering lips. "The way he looked at me." She shook her head as tears filled her eyes. "Those eyes haunt me. I see them all the time. I feel his hands touching me. With one look, I was back in that house."

"And you got out again."

Allie nodded. "He said he'd give me the name for a kiss."

"I'm guessing Marcus had something to say about that."

Allie nodded. "He refused to let me do it."

"But you were stubborn." Dr. Seaver said knowingly.

Again she nodded and sighed, rubbing her upper arms. "I'd already considered he might do that. There was a bowl of candy in the reception area so I grabbed some candy from there and I gave him a kiss, just not the one he was expecting."

Dr. Seaver chuckled. "I'm sure that didn't go over well."

"Not with him, but Marcus sure liked it." Allie sighed and shook her head. "I wish I had never gone. I barely got any sleep last night, even with my guard dog in the other room."

"You have a dog?"

Allie smiled. "Marcus. He's still sleeping on the couch to make sure I'm all right."

"Ah, yes. Does he know about all of this? Does he know you came here?"

"No, I snuck out this morning. I couldn't tell him."

"Why not?"

"What if we need more information from Bastian? I'll have to go back. He won't be satisfied talking to Marcus anymore." Allie licked her lips. "I'm just not sure if I could prepare on my own if I did have to go back. I'll need help and I figured you'd be the best person to help me prepare for my second meeting with him."

"There really shouldn't be any more meetings with him, Allie, not until you've had time to process everything. Physically he didn't do you any harm, but it's obvious you're mentally and emotionally unstable." He held up his hand to stop her before she could speak. "I'm not saying you're crazy or anything. I'm just saying you've been through a mental and emotional trauma. They are worse than physical trauma's. It takes time."

Allie rubbed her face in her hands. "I don't have time." Allie motioned toward the window. "There is a man out there killing people. He has to be stopped and Bastian has all of that information. I have to go to him!"

"No you don't. You don't have to do all of this alone, Allie. It's okay to let Marcus do it. If Bastian won't talk to him, then you can both figure out something else to do. You're a good detective, Allie, and so is Marcus. You guys can find this guy. You don't *need* this Bastian character to solve cases. You didn't need him before and you certainly don't need him now."

Allie nodded slowly. He was right. Bastian was cocky because he thought they needed him and they couldn't do this without him, but he was wrong. She and Marcus had the best closure rate in the city. They would find this killer and put him in a cell with Bastian. This was not the end. Allie looked up at the doctor. "Thank you." She stood up and shook his hand. "I have to get back to the house before Marcus wakes up. We have a new case."

Dr. Seaver stood and walked her to the door. "Take care of yourself, Allie. My door is always open for you."

12

7 Days to Election Day

"Mrs. Albright, I'm Detective Krenshaw, this is Detective Marcus." Allie shook Mrs. Albright's hand. "We're sorry for your loss."

Mrs. Albright nodded and held a tissue to her nose as she sniffed. "I just can't believe it's actually happened. I just saw Evan two days ago and we were planning our twenty-fifth wedding anniversary." She pursed her lips and looked at Allie. "We always wanted to go on an Alaskan cruise. I hear it's the best one to go on. Evan isn't really the cruise type. He was just going for me."

Allie glanced over at Marcus before looking back at Mrs. Albright. "Mrs. Albright, did you husband have any enemies?"

"Oh, call me Jane." She held the tissue to her nose and sniffed once more.

Marcus nudged her and she looked up at him. He stared at her with raised eyebrows. He was thinking the same thing she was. There was something odd about the tissue Mrs. Albright kept sniffing.

"It says here you were out of town the morning your husband was killed. Where were you, Jane?"

The woman's eyes grew large and she leaned forward. "Am I a suspect?"

She seemed almost excited at the thought and Allie found herself making eye contact with Marcus once more. "No, Jane, we are just attempting to verify where you were." Marcus explained.

"Oh, well yes, I was out of town."

Allie bit her lip and cleared her throat. "Yes, Jane, but where were you?"

"Canada."

Allie cleared her throat again. She could feel Marcus' eyes on her. "Right, well Jane, can you tell me if your husband had any enemies?"

"Oh I'm sure he did, but he wouldn't have let me associate with them. They'd probably do something to me to get to him. He was very protective, my Evan was." She sniffed the tissue again.

"Right, well can you tell me what exactly kind of work Evan was into?"

"Of course! He was unemployed."

Allie frowned and glanced at Marcus before looking at Jane. "So are you working, then?"

"Oh no, my Evan never would let me work."

"Are you getting benefits from the government, then?"

"Oh no, my Evan didn't take handouts."

Marcus chuckled and leaned forward, covering Jane's tissue with his hand. "Jane, what my partner is trying to understand is how you came to have money for food and this trip you took to Canada."

"Oh, I'm rich. My father died leaving a hefty fortune behind." She went to sniff the tissue again but Marcus stopped her. She didn't seem to mind. "And my Evan and I we didn't have any children, never could conceive, so we get all of the money to ourselves." She giggled and raised the tissue to her nose. This time Marcus let her.

Allie bit her lip and raised her eyebrows in Marcus' direction. "Well, Jane, can you tell me when the last time Evan had his car worked on?" She made eye contact with the woman again. Her eyes had a glassy look to them and Allie wondered what room they should confine the woman to.

"Oh, I'm not sure. I don't know that he ever got the car worked on. I didn't know we had a car!" She giggled and sniffed the tissue again.

"Here, let me get you a fresh tissue." Marcus easily made the switch with her. He took her tissue and tossed it in the trashcan.

Jane's eyes were glued to the trashcan.

"All right, Jane, I guess since you don't know who would want your husband dead and he didn't work, then there isn't much more we could ask you." Allie stopped and looked at the petite woman in front of her. Nate had told her before he only killed people he was asked to and while she couldn't see him crawling under a car, you could never be sure. "Jane, did you kill your husband?"

"Oh, no I was in Canada." She pursed her lips and bobbed her head up and down as if that would assure them of her innocence.

"Right. Well, did you have him killed?"

"Have him killed?"

"Did you hire someone to kill your husband for you?"

Her eyes grew large. "You can do that?"

"Yes, Jane, now will you please answer the question? Did you hire someone to kill your husband?"

"Well, I should say not! I wouldn't!" She lifted her chin a notch. She went to sniff her tissue then stopped, frowned at it and stuffed it in her purse.

Allie stood up and went to stand in front of Marcus. "I guess it's no fun sniffing police tissues."

"I guess not, though I've enjoyed it from time to time." He smiled down at her. "Want me to take it from here?"

"Please. We'll never get anything out of her in this state. Charging her?"

"Definitely."

"Good." Allie turned back to Jane. "Jane, Detective Marcus is going to take you down the hall. He has a few more things to discuss with you. If you think of anything that might help, just let me know, all right?"

Jane's head bobbed up and down, her eyes going back to the trashcan.

Allie spun on her heel and looked at Marcus with raised eyebrows. "She's all yours." Allie patted him on the shoulder and left, thankful she didn't have to deal with that. She made her way to her desk and had been sitting only a second before her phone rang. "Krenshaw."

"Allie, it's Dana. You and Marcus need to come down here."

"All right. We'll be there in about ten minutes." Allie hung up and called to Marcus. "Make it quick, Dana has something for us."

Marcus nodded and ushered Jane down the hall.

Allie glanced over at Captain Ashton's office. Megan was lying on the couch, her eyes staring up at the ceiling. Allie stood so she could see Ashton. He was on the phone. She went over to the door and poked her head in. Ashton looked up at her and she pointed at Megan. Ashton nodded and started yelling at the person on the phone.

"Megan, come on."

Not having to be told twice, Megan hurried from the room. She sighed. "Thank you. I am bored out of my mind. Since Mr. Bradley realized I was following him and filed a complaint, I've been keeping Ashton company."

"Do you know him? I mean, other than him being your boss."

"My dad is a fireman and he plays golf with Captain Ashton, has for years." Megan put her hands on her hips. "So where are we off to?"

"Marcus is taking care of something and we are heading to get some information from Dana.

You looked like you might be interested in tagging along."

"Yes! Please!" Megan went over to her desk and took out her cell phone and a pack of gum. "Want a piece?"

"No thanks." Allie glanced around and spotted Marcus heading their way. "Ready to go?"

"Yep!" Megan slipped her cell phone in her back pocket and followed Allie to the elevator.

"The three musketeers are back!" Marcus smiled and glanced over at Megan. "How are you feeling?"

"Fine, considering I was stabbed and robbed. How are you feeling?"

"Fine, considering I was blown up." Marcus grinned and looked at Allie. "How are you feeling?"

"Nauseated." She said dryly and stepped into the elevator. "Come on you two comedians, time to play cop."

*****

He was ahead of the game, for once in his life. Allie and her partners had just gotten Evan Albright's body, meaning they finally figured out it was a homicide. He was afraid he was going to have to go downtown and confess before they gave him credit for it. Al needed to know how many votes were being lost.

Tony whistled as he crossed the street. He stopped on the sidewalk, frowning at the campaign sign in the front yard. He shook his head and went up to the porch. He could take care of the sign later. There were more pressing matters to attend to. Tony skipped up the steps and knocked on the door.

A teenaged girl answered the door. "Yeah?"

"Is your mother home?"

"Yeah." She glanced up from her phone to holler for her mother over her shoulder. She then looked back down at her phone.

"Who is it, Becky?"

Becky made a face. "How should I know?" Becky sauntered away and her mother appeared in the doorway.

"Good evening, are you Roberta Kentlee?"

"I am, Bobbi Kentlee. How can I help you?"

Tony beamed. "I'm here for the Dan Norton campaign and I just have a few questions for you. Would you mind if I came in and interviewed you?"

"Oh, well, um, could we just do it here?" Bobbi smiled, leaning against the doorjamb. "It's not a long interview, is it?"

"No, no, it isn't." Tony cleared his throat and heard someone coming up behind him. He glanced over his shoulder and saw Bobbi's oldest, Michael, coming up the walkway.

"Mom, I'm hungry. Do we have food?" He swung his baseball bat up to rest on his shoulder and waited for Bobbi to move out of his way.

"Pizza is still in the oven. Go in and change and it'll be ready." Bobbi pushed away from the doorjamb.

This was his chance. Tony grabbed the baseball bat, hooked it under Michael's chin, choking him just enough to get everyone's attention. "Let's have that interview inside." He told a terrified Bobbi.

"Please, let him go."

"Inside." Tony urged them both into the house and closed the door behind them. He was almost glad Bobbi hadn't let him in. If he had gotten started early, he would have missed Michael and that would've been sad. He would've had a witness to track down. This way, he had a nice, clean getaway.

*****

"I thought you guys should see this." Dana walked them over to the car and pointed at the back seat. "I guess no one thought to make the connection, but I knew what you were both working on.

Marcus pulled on some gloves and opened the door. In the backseat of Evan Albright's car was a yard campaign sign and a small stack of flyers announcing the upcoming election. Marcus pulled the sign out and showed it to Allie. "Well, I guess it's safe to say we can add this one to our pile."

Allie took the sign and shook her head. "I can't believe this. It's getting ridiculous! Why can't we catch this guy! He's obviously an amateur and scary as it may sound, he seems to be enjoying it."

"So what do we do?" Megan asked. "Shouldn't we warn people about this? Maybe we can get people to take down the campaign signs from their yard."

"I have a feeling he already has his victims picked out. We've got to find his list." Allie looked at Marcus. "I'm going to go out and find Nate."

"Shawn."

"Yeah, whatever his name is. See what you can find about his family. It may just take a killer to find a killer." Allie threw the sign into the backseat of the car and headed outside. There had to be a way to draw Nate out into the open. Last time, it took someone wanting to kill her. Maybe it was time to make another trip to prison to visit Bastian, this time by herself.

13

5 days to Election Day

"We've got another one. This time, I know it's connected." Marcus hurried over to Allie's desk and handed her the new file. "Bobbi Kentlee."

"How do I know that name?" Allie frowned up at him.

"Probably from TV. She was a reporter. She was doing a lot of the campaign coverage. She did a piece on Dan Norton that was quite impressive. It turned things around for him." Marcus flipped open the file. "The strange part is this. He killed both of her kids and set it up to look like she killed them then killed herself."

"He hasn't staged the scenes before. Are we sure it's connected and not murder/suicide?" Allie glanced over the crime scene photos.

"Oh I'm sure." Marcus flipped through the pictures and put one on top. "See that?"

"The black smudge?" Allie frowned. "So there's a stain on the carpet."

"Not a stain, that's a footprint, I'm sure of it. The rest of this house is spotless. If there was a footprint or stain on the carpet, Bobbi would have cleaned it up immediately. She's a perfectionist."

"Did you know her on a more personal level?" Allie smiled up at him. "You sure seem to know an awful lot about her."

Marcus grinned. "We went on a date."

"Just one?"

"Oh yeah."

"Why just one? She was pretty."

"Because she was a perfectionist and it drove me nuts!" Marcus closed the file. "Let's go to her house and see what we can find. I will bet you dinner tonight that it's connected and we'll find evidence of that as soon as we step foot in that house."

Allie nodded. "I'll take that bet. Winner buys and picks the food."

"Deal." Marcus shook her hand and called over to Megan. "You want in."

"Sure!" Megan came over. "In on what?"

Marcus rolled his eyes. "Never mind. We're heading to a crime scene. Saddle up, let's ride!" He grabbed up the file from Allie's desk and hurried to the elevator. He had about fifteen minutes to figure out what he wanted for dinner tonight.

*****

"I knew you wouldn't be hard to find." Allie stopped at the entrance to the prison and looked at the security guard leaning against the gate. "You couldn't resist protecting me."

The security guard pushed away from the gate and stepped toward her. He raised his head and smiled at her. She could recognize those baby blue eyes and dimpled smile anywhere. Nate Harris. "You caught me."

"So tell me, do you prefer Nate or Shawn?"

His eyes grew large and he looked around quickly, keeping his back to the wall. "Where did you hear that name?"

"An informant." Allie frowned and looked around as well. "What are you expecting? A hit squad to come take me down because I uttered the name Shawn?"

"Stop saying that. I mean it. Tell me you haven't done any research on that name."

Allie shook her head. "No, but Marcus is."

"Call him now. Tell him to stop." His eyes locked with hers. She'd never seen him his serious or this scared, not even when he was bleeding out in closet.

Allie pulled out her phone and called Marcus. "Marcus, you need to stop researching him. I've got him right now. He's standing right in front of me."

"Seriously?" Marcus exclaimed. "Where are you? I'll be there in a minute."

"No. Something's not right. Just stop whatever research you're doing." Allie kept her eyes on Nate. His gaze never wavered from hers. Something was happening.

"Allie, the man is a killer. You can't do this on your own. It's just a trick of his."

"No it isn't. Trust me, Marcus." Allie hung up the phone and slipped it in her back pocket. "All right, now he doesn't trust me and is mad. What's the deal?"

"Why are you guys trying to find me?"

Allie scoffed. "Uh, maybe because you're a murderer? Wouldn't that be your first clue?"

"I haven't killed anyone." Nate hesitated and winced. "Recently."

"Were you hired to kill Evan Albright?"

Nate shook his head. "I don't know who that is."

"We're trying to find the man who you claim was attempting to kill me."

Nate nodded, his eyes still scanning the perimeter. "Yes, he put the bomb in your car and was going to shoot you at the mayor's office but I stopped him. He's not the sharpest tool in the shed. He does seem to know how to cover his tracks, I'll give him that."

"Wait, he planted the bomb in my car too? Did he stab Megan?"

Nate's eyes met hers. "Megan? I don't know a Megan."

"I've been working with her. She's a little taller than me, short brown hair and bright makeup. She's actually pretty cute. Your type, I would think."

The corner of his mouth hitched up in a smile. "You think you know my type?"

"I have a pretty good idea." She said, biting her bottom lip.

"Well, I do know who the girl is and no, he's not the one that stabbed her. I did."

Allie's mouth dropped open. "Excuse me? *You* stabbed Megan?" She exclaimed and reached for her handcuffs. "You'll burn for this."

"Relax. I didn't kill her. You know I could have if I wanted to. I was *supposed* to kill her but I knew she was your friend so I didn't. I missed all of the major organs; it was basically a flesh wound. Don't be so dramatic." Nate sighed and continued scanning the perimeter. He didn't seem at all concerned about her knowledge of his indiscretion. Why didn't that bother him?

"That's still a crime. It's attempted murder."

"I don't *attempt* to murder people, Allie. I either do or I don't. End of story." Nate sighed. "Was there anything else or are you going to go visit your boyfriend so I can get out of the line of fire?"

"This is a prison. Someone would be crazy to take a shot at you here."

"Yeah, crazy or a cop." Nate looked her up and down in one swift move. "That's not why *you're* here is it?"

Allie made a face. "Really? If anything I should be arresting you right now, but you've intrigued me."

"Have I?" Nate wiggled his eyebrows.

Allie laughed and playfully pushed him away. "Seriously though, why do you think a cop would kill you?"

"Why *wouldn't* a cop try to kill me?"

"Forget it." Allie sighed and pulled her small notebook from her pocket. "I do have a few questions for you about the guy you met."

"All right, but make them quick."

"Would you rather go talk in my car?"

"No, I feel safer here." He smiled, his eyes teasing.

"Funny. It's Marcus' car."

"Oh, well then I *really* feel safer here." Nate leaned against the building, his eyes scanning around them. "First question."

"Did you know him?"

"No. I asked him what he was doing and he said it wasn't any of my business. I told him to stay away from you. That's about the size of it. Your SWAT team would be breathing down my neck soon so I had to get out of there."

"Yes, after leaving your gun behind. Thanks for the note, by the way."

"You're welcome." He looked at her long enough to wink then continued his surveillance. "You didn't show it to anyone, did you?"

"Just Marcus."

Nate nodded. "That's good. Keep it between us."

"All right. You really don't trust cops, do you?"

"No, just you and Marcus." He tilted his head back and forth. "And I guess I could trust Megan. She seems to be a sweet kid. A little naïve, but sweet. It was almost too easy getting that bag from her."

"Yeah, about that. Who hired you to do that?"

"I actually don't know. I got my assignment but I never got the name of the client. I dropped it off with my superior and that was it." Nate shook his head. "The whole thing was weird, different than any job I've had in the past. I guess that's partly why I didn't kill Megan too."

"So this guy you talked to, what did he look like?"

"Well, honestly, he was kind of deformed almost."

"Deformed?"

"Yeah, like he'd been in a fire or an accident or something. His face and hands were all scarred and he walks with a bit of a limp, but not all the time. I'm thinking he has an artificial leg and probably a bad hip. He may have been in a car accident or something to get that."

"Which leg?"

"Right." Nate frowned. "He really isn't the best. I mean, he was right out there in the open. I could have shot him instead of you."

"And why didn't you?" Allie raised her eyebrows in question.

"Well because then you'd be after me, wouldn't you?" Nate smiled and glanced over at her. "Not that I wouldn't want you to chase after me, but the end result probably wouldn't be as pleasant as I'm imagining."

Allie smiled. "You never know. You might be surprised." Allie made a few notes in her notebook. "What color eyes did he have? Hair color? Was he tall?"

"He was Marcus' height, or pretty close to it. He had Marcus' build, but he goes to the kitchen more than the gym. Brown eyes and blond hair. If I were a betting man, I would say he lived somewhere near the mayor's office."

"Why do you say that?"

"He carried a black bag that you could easily see concealed a gun. If he went too far with that, it would have drawn attention and he probably couldn't have gotten a cab with it so he has to be within walking distance. With his limp, he wouldn't have been able to walk very far. Thus, he probably lived within a two block radius of the mayor's office."

"You're really good at this. You should have become a cop."

Nate smiled. "The only reason I am so good at this is because I've been hiding from cops most of my life." He glanced over at her. "Any other questions?"

"Do you want to have dinner with me tomorrow night?" Allie looked up at him. This time she had his full attention.

"Really?"

"Is that too hard of a question?" She smiled up at him and waited.

He smiled, showing off his dimples. "I want to say yes."

"But?"

"But I can't."

"Why not?"

Nate took a deep breath and sighed. "Because I don't want to get any further on Marcus' bad list than I already am. You really need to talk to him about his hate issues. Tell him I said to hate the crime, not the criminal." Nate winked and started away from her.

"He's not going to want to hear that."

"Then just give him my love." Nate turned around, kissed his hand and tossed his hand up in the air.

Allie shook her head, watching him jump in a black BMW convertible and drive away. If the man weren't a criminal, she could see herself dating him. Sadly, he was a criminal, and the worst kind. He was a charming criminal. Marcus would not be happy to hear she spoke face to face with him then let him drive away unharmed. Maybe one day Marcus would come around and see in Nate what she saw. Nate was a trapped man and he just wanted his freedom. One day she would find the person who held the key to his chains and she'd set him free once and for all.

14

4 Days to Election Day

Marcus sat with Megan and tried to be as cool as possible despite Allie's need to go off on investigations without him. If he had been there when Nate had shown up at the prison, he would have arrested him, no questions asked until he was in interrogation.

He knew he should be thankful Nate had managed to keep her from talking to Bastian and he had been good enough to answer some major questions, but he wasn't. Nate was a killer who deserved to be behind bars, especially after learning what he did to Megan. How could Allie just let him walk away? Why did she trust him?

"All right, let's lay out what we *do* know about this guy starting with the first crime scene which would be the Gilmore's." Allie pointed to the bulletin board where she pinned up her typical note cards. Office supply stores would never go out of business as long as Allie was alive. "Megan, you had the Gilmore's. Break it down for us."

Megan pulled out her phone and cleared her throat. "All right, I asked my dad a lot of questions about this to be sure I understood it all right. He said that the fire at the Gilmore's was set intentionally. It was started in the bedroom but there was another fire started in the closet where, Allie, you said you found the wire that we have now discovered are sign holders. It was a cocktail that started the fire. There was a partially melted plastic bottle found in the bedroom. Dad said the fire in the closet was most likely set and then the killer went outside and threw the cocktail into the bedroom window."

"It was a plastic bottle?"

Megan nodded. "That's what Dad said. He thought it was odd too because usually they use glass so it breaks open and spreads everywhere. However, there were all kinds of accelerant all over that house. The fire would have been able to go for quite a while. Mr. and Mrs. Gilmore had signs of blunt force trauma found on their heads which appear to be caused by each other's head. Dana did some checking on that and it was confirmed last night."

"So the killer breaks in, bashes their heads together, sets their closet ablaze and then goes outside to set the second fire? Why would he do that? It makes no sense." Marcus shook his head.

"If he was already in the house, why wouldn't he start it in the kitchen or something? Why the bedroom?"

Allie picked up a notecard and wrote 'why bedroom' and pinned it to the bulletin board. "Good question, we'll come back to it. Next is the Lancaster's. Marcus, you had that one."

"All right, well, it appears the family was just sitting down to dinner when the killer came in. Because everyone was in the same room, you can assume that they were about to eat and were interrupted. The killer came in and there was a struggle by the front door. I'm assuming he struggled with Mrs. Lancaster, otherwise there would have been more of a struggle in the dining room where the family was found."

"What do you mean? Allie and I figured Mr. Lancaster answered the door." Megan opened a new notepad on her phone, ready to jot down what he said.

Marcus nodded. "That's what I thought at first glance, but if that was the case, why didn't the woman get her children to safety? With the woman answering the door and being attacked, the man would immediately go to the aid of his wife because he knows he has a better chance of subduing the man than his wife does. His thought is to take the man down to save his family where as his wife would be ready to get the children out and not to stand and fight."

Megan nodded. "Okay, so the man attacks the killer. How does the killer manage to subdue them both?"

"The man goes to the aid of his wife and the killer's only chance of getting out of it is to turn the wife and use her as leverage." Marcus asked Megan to stand up, facing away from him. He wrapped his arm around her neck, holding her securely. "If I grab you like this and hold you against me, you can't get free."

Allie stepped in. "As her husband, I would want to do something but I couldn't do it without running the risk of hurting her in the process so I don't do anything."

"Exactly." Marcus released Megan and leaned against the desk again. "So he kills them all. He tied them all up, maybe even having the children tie up their parents. The children were killed quickly. He took pity on them. The mother he killed fast too, but the father, he didn't. His focus was on the man and made him suffer more."

Allie wrote up a notecard and hung it up under the Lancaster's name. 'Man suffered more'. "All right, anything else on that one?"

Marcus shook his head. "Nope. You're up for Jenna."

"All right, there's not a lot about what happened to her. We know she left the club with a man. I talked to her friend who said she never got a good look at the guy, but said that Jenna felt sorry for him and that's why she was hanging out with him."

"Why did she feel sorry for him?" Megan paused her typing to ask.

"Well, from what Nate told me about him, the guy has scars like he was in a fire and he walks with a limp, so maybe she felt bad about his appearance because she thought maybe he couldn't get a girl? I don't know."

"And we're getting this from a professional liar and serial killer." Marcus rolled his eyes and sighed. "This is ridiculous. We need to just forget about everything Nate said. How do we know he isn't the one doing all of this?"

"Nate has had more than one chance to kill me and he hasn't. He said he was supposed to kill Megan but he didn't so I'm willing to give him the benefit of a doubt."

"He's a liar, Allie! Spinning stories like this is what he does for a living. Why should we trust him at all?" Marcus scoffed and shook his head. "I mean, really. If I lied to you once you wouldn't believe me ever again. You'd be holding that above my head, taking every word I said with a grain of salt, but this guy you entrust everything to. Help me understand why."

"He helped me. He didn't have to. He could have killed me and ended all of his problems but he didn't. He's been a friend to me and I trust him." Allie shrugged. "You'd have to see him, to look him in the face and you'd believe him too. He trusts you."

"Because I'm a trustworthy person. I can keep a secret. I don't lie. I'm a good person. I can't say the same about him." Marcus shook his head. "You're going to end up regretting this, Allie."

"Well, when that time comes, I'll let you say 'I told you so', but until then, let's focus on this case." Allie pointed to some notecards on the bulletin board. "He has the scars, blond hair and brown eyes. He is Marcus' height and build and he doesn't appear to work out."

Marcus leaned over to Megan. "You might make a note in there that these are observations of a known serial killer."

If Allie heard him, she was choosing to ignore his comment. "It's estimated that he lived within a two block radius of the mayor's office."

"So what do we do? Start knocking on doors?"

"No. We need to narrow the list down." Marcus stood up and looked at the map of the city, focusing on the area within the red circle Allie had drawn on it. "I can call Scott and have him pull up people living in that area. We can narrow it down by sex, hair color and eye color and then maybe we won't have as many doors to knock on. Maybe one of the names will stick out to us."

"Good. Get a hold of Scott. Megan and I will look into Bobbi Kentlee and do some more searching on Evan Albright. We don't have a lot to go on with him. I'd like to go talk to his wife again. Hopefully she's sober."

Marcus nodded. "Don't we all. I'll call you if we find anything." Marcus grabbed the keys off his desk as he headed to the elevator. He had to find something. Part of him wanted Nate to be wrong about all of this. But if Nate was wrong, that meant they were still weeks away from finding their killer and the election was only four days away. They were racing against the clock on this one.

*****

Allie walked into the Kentlee house. She crouched down next to the foot prints on the carpet that had cost her dinner two nights ago. It was odd that this footprint had gotten left behind yet there was nothing like this at the other crime scenes. What was different about this one? Was it the children? No, he'd killed children before.

"Hey, I found something here." Megan called and brought over a used facial tissue. "This was in the trash over there, but there's a hair on it."

"That could be anyone's hair. Bobbi or one of the kids could have used that."

"True, but can't we still get it looked at just to be sure?"

Her protégé seemed to be grasping at straws, but maybe not. "What makes it stand out to you?"

Megan nodded toward the trashcan. "It was the only thing in that trashcan. All of the other trashcans in the house have a plastic liner in them but that one doesn't. It also doesn't match anything in this room which makes me think that maybe it doesn't belong here. What if it's a trashcan that Bobbi was going to get rid of? The killer wouldn't know this, so blowing his nose or whatever and throwing it in that trashcan wouldn't have been a big deal."

Allie nodded. "Good point. Bag it and we'll take it to Dana."

Megan's smile stretched across her face. "Great! Thanks!" She looked around at the floor where Allie was. "What are you looking at?"

"The footprints."

"Why?"

"He made a mistake. Possibly two if what you say about that tissue is true." Allie shook her head and glanced around the room. "Something about all of this changed for him when he saw this family. Bobbi was a widow, right?"

"Right. Her husband was a Marine and he was killed overseas two years ago."

Military. Allie stood up and looked around the room for pictures. She spotted three. The one on the book shelf was a picture of Bobbi with her children. It would have been too far away for the killer to see. She went back, placing her feet right next to the prints he'd left behind. From here, she looked around the room. Finally, she spotted it. He hadn't seen a picture.

"He saw the flag."

"What?"

Allie pointed at the triangle folded flag on the shelf in the corner. "That's probably the flag Bobbi was given at her husband's funeral. It sparked something with him."

"You think he was military?"

Allie nodded and pulled out her phone to dial Marcus. "It might explain the scars he had and the limp."

"Marcus."

"Hey, check for a military background. I'm at the Kentlee's and she has her husband's flag on display in the front room." Allie heard Marcus mumble something. "We'll keep checking. Let me know if you find anything."

"Will do. We're just getting started though."

Allie hung up and pocketed her phone. "All right, let's get out of here. We need to go to Evan

Albright's house. We need to find out what he was doing for money." Allie locked the door behind them and went down to her borrowed squad car.

"I thought his wife was independently wealthy."

"She is, but that doesn't mean he didn't have a job. Some men have pride and want to work."

"And you think Evan was one of them."

Allie shrugged. "I have hope in all men. It's one of my flaws, I guess." Allie winked and sat down behind the wheel.

"Does it ever scare you to get in a car since yours blew up?"

Allie scoffed. "Yeah, I guess I didn't really think about it. I mean, Marcus was the one getting in the car when it happened, not me. And Nate said he talked to the guy and I know Nate has my back."

Allie backed the car out of the driveway and headed down the block, looking around the neighborhood. She spotted at least four curious neighbors. That meant she could possibly have four witnesses to question.

"How do you know?"

"How do I know what?"

"How do you know Nate has your back? That you can trust him? I mean, he shot you and stabbed me." Megan shrugged. "I have to agree with Marcus on this one. The man doesn't seem very trustworthy."

Allie winced and shrugged. "I don't know. You'd just have to talk to him. There's just something about him that puts me at ease. He kind of reminds me of my brother."

"I didn't know you had a brother."

"He was a cop. Worked undercover in narcotics. Someone came in and killed his entire crew. They never found the guy who did it." Allie frowned, her mind slowly putting pieces together. "But they were all shot in the back of the head, execution style."

Nate's signature.

"I'm sorry." Megan smiled and nudged Allie's arm as she attempted to lighten the mood. "I did talk to him a little bit. He's *really* cute."

Allie laughed lightly. "Yes, he is. Just don't ever let Marcus hear you say that. He'd give you quite a tongue-lashing and you'd have to hear the story about how Nate locked him in the bathroom and ruined his self-esteem."

"He locked Marcus in a bathroom?"

Allie nodded, glad to have someone to share in her amusement. "At the hospital. I told Marcus he should just be thankful Nate let him live. Oh, that really got him going."

"So is that why he doesn't like him?"

"No. The two of them never really got along very well, not from the moment Nate first started working with us. Marcus just kept saying he didn't trust the guy." Allie shrugged. "Marcus and I rarely disagree, but we did on that." Allie slowed and squinted to read a street sign. "Did we pass his house?"

"I don't think so." Megan looked at her phone. "No, his house is on the next block. You're good."

Allie's phone vibrated in her pocket. She pulled it out. "It's Marcus." Allie set her phone on the dash and pushed the green button, immediately turning on the speaker phone. "Marcus, you're on speaker with me and Megan."

"We found him and you are never going to believe who it is."

15

3 Days to Election Day

"I demand to know why you brought me in here. I have three days until the election and I am behind in the polls!" Kent Bradley paced back and forth in Captain Ashton's office. "When will you release my son?"

"After he's answered some questions, Mr. Bradley, and not until he's answered them." Ashton took the picture Allie handed him. "Your son's apartment has windows directly across the street from Mayor Norton's office. My detectives found some things in his apartment. The thing I found the most interesting was this sniper rifle! We asked him where he got it and he lawyered up and called you. Maybe you can talk some sense into him."

"My son didn't do this." Kent had sobered quickly after seeing the rifle. "He's a sniper in the Army. He just got back from his second tour."

"Which is another thing that drew our attention. Did you know that Detective Krenshaw here was shot by a sniper from the top of your son's apartment building?"

Kent's head snapped to her. He met her eyes. "Is that true?"

Allie lifted her shirt sleeve to reveal the bandage on her left arm. "It's very true. Do you want to go talk to your son now?"

Kent pursed his lips and nodded. "If you wouldn't mind."

"I'll take you to him." Allie opened the door and led Kent down the hall to the interrogation room that held his son. She knocked on the door twice and opened it. Marcus looked at her with raised eyebrows. "His father is here to speak to him." Marcus stood and left the room without question.

"I'd like this to be a private conversation."

"We won't be listening in, if that's what you mean. The cameras in this room will stay plugged in and recording, though."

Kent nodded. "Fair enough." Kent went to sit in the chair Marcus had vacated. Kent's son wouldn't even look up from the table. He'd been sitting straight up for the last two hours they'd had him in the box. Sooner or later his composure would have to give a little.

Allie closed the door and went to lean against the desk with Marcus. She studied the bulletin board. "It just doesn't make sense."

"What doesn't?"

"He's killing candidates so his father would win? He just got out of a war zone. Why would he create one here?"

"Post-traumatic stress?" Marcus shrugged. "It could be any number of things. Maybe he had begun to enjoy the violence he saw over there and missed it. War does crazy things to people."

Allie nodded. "Yeah, but would post-traumatic stress and his need for violence keep him organized? I mean, he didn't do a wonderful job of it, it was all pretty sloppy, but those footprints at Kentlee's house mean something big. When he saw that flag, something changed in him. I don't think this kid could have those feelings just by seeing that flag."

"Have you talked to Nate? Maybe you should show him the kid's picture."

"You want me to talk to him?" Allie frowned up at Marcus. "So now you trust him?"

"Not at all, but so far, he's been the best witness, the only witness, we've had on this case. And it's like you said, it takes a killer to catch a killer." Marcus sighed. "If I have to arrest a man in uniform, I want to make sure there isn't even the slightest possibility he could be innocent."

Allie nodded. "I agree. I'll see if I can't draw Nate out again. He probably knows about the arrest already. He'll be ready to answer questions, I think."

"Let's hope."

*****

Two more days and his job was done. Tony sat in his car, watching the Prescott family. This would be his final statement, the big finale. A small smile lifted the corners of his mouth. It was the final countdown.

Killing Bobbi and her children still weighed heavily on his mind. Seeing her husband's shrine in the corner had taken him back to his time served. Joining the Army hadn't been his choice. He'd been forced to join, but it was the most meaningful thing he'd ever done in his life. Killing that family had been necessary to his cause, but it felt as if he'd betrayed his brother.

Tony glanced down at the dog tags in his hand. He clenched his fist around them and gritted his teeth. "They died for a good cause." Jerking the car door handle, he got out, slammed the door shut and marched up to the house. He slipped the dog tags into his pocket and pulled the gun out from the back of his pants.

"The final countdown." He kicked in the front door of the house, screams echoing in the night.

*****

"Don't go in there." Marcus rested his hands on Allie's shoulders. "It's really not worth it. All you need to know is this man is a psychopath."

Allie took a deep breath. "How many?"

"Five."

Allie's eyes slammed shut. The body count was up to sixteen. Why hadn't she been able to stop this guy? He could already be out there stalking his next victim and she was still cleaning up his last four messes. "How did it happen?"

"Shot."

Her eyes snapped open and she looked up at him. "How were they shot?"

Marcus shook his head. "It wasn't Nate. The door was kicked in. It looks like he just kicked the door down and started firing until no one else moved. I hate the man, but Nate would never do something so distasteful."

Allie released a sigh of relief. "Good." She still wondered if he'd had a part in her brother's killing. After connecting the pieces with Megan yesterday, she hadn't been able to stop thinking about it. What if Nate had killed her brother? Allie pushed the thought aside. "Did you see anything connecting this?"

Marcus nodded. "The family itself. Husband, wife, three children. Tell me if this sounds familiar. Husband is a stand-up family man, works a simple full time job in one of the corporate offices downtown. His wife is on the school board. She is a special education teacher. The three children are all under the age of ten. They all have perfect grades. They have a family dinner every night, a large family dinner on Sunday afternoons with his parents."

"Should that sound familiar?"

Marcus pulled out his phone, clicked a few buttons and handed it to her.

Allie found herself looking at an article about Dan Norton. She frowned and started scrolling through the article. It was all about him, his wife and their three children. Everything Marcus had just told her matched up almost perfectly with Dan Norton. Allie swallowed hard. "This is the ultimatum. He's telling Mayor Norton if he doesn't back out of the race this is what will happen to his family."

Marcus nodded, his face grim. "They all had masks on when first responders got here."

She hated to ask, but she had to. "What kind of masks?"

"A cutout of Dan Norton's face."

A chill went down her spine. "Well, I guess this proves it wasn't Jonathan Bradley."

Marcus gave a stiff nod. "My thoughts exactly. I'm going to call and get him released."

"I think I'd better go down to Mayor Norton's office and let him know what's going on. Election Day is two days from now. Tomorrow the candidates will be having their big celebrations. If this guy is planning to kill Mayor Norton, he may try to do it at this big party." Allie pulled out her phone and dialed Mayor Norton's office on her way to the squad car.

"Allie."

Allie moved the mouthpiece away from her mouth. "What?"

Marcus' face softened. He gulped and tilted his head to the side as he winced. "Just, be careful, okay?"

She lifted the corner of her mouth in a smile. "I will." With that he seemed to relax a bit before he disappeared inside the house.

"Mayor Norton's office."

Allie turned her attention to her phone call. "This is Detective Krenshaw. I am on my way to your office now. I need to speak with Mayor Norton immediately."

16

Election Day

Marcus met Allie outside the door of the mayor's office. "This makes no sense. Everything is pointing to Mayor Norton as a target. We have men everywhere but no one has spotted anyone resembling this guy." Marcus ran his hand through his hair. "I don't know what else to do."

Allie nodded. "We'll figure it out. We always do."

"How is the mayor taking all of this?"

"He's mad." Allie shrugged. "Now ask me how much I care."

Marcus chuckled and looked up and down the hallway. "This entire floor is cleared. We are stretched pretty thin trying to keep a close eye on voting booths. I just hope he hasn't somehow planted a bomb in any of them."

"What do you think will happen if Mayor Norton gets re-elected?"

"I would rather *not* think about it." Marcus pulled out his phone. He missed a call from Megan. "Keep the mayor in the inner office with his family. I'll have some food brought up to them. Meanwhile, you just stay safe, all right?"

"Would you relax? I'm not a china doll, you know."

Marcus gripped her wrist, preventing her from walking away from him. He pulled her close, his face mere inches from hers. He studied her eyes before his gaze rested on her lips. His heart beat violently inside his chest. He lowered his head, covering her lips with his. He felt her body relax as he wrapped his arm around her waist and held her close.

He reluctantly broke the kiss. Her eyes locked with his. "Stop arguing and do as I say. I want to be able to do that again sometime." He smiled and stepped back. He held eye contact for just a moment longer before he turned and started down the hall. "The mayor is waiting, Allie." He called over his shoulder. He heard her gasp and fumble with the door handle. He couldn't stop the satisfied smile the stretched across his face. Two years of waiting and it was definitely worth it.

*****

"It's finally here!" Tony skipped to the kitchen and started to prepare his breakfast. His cat sat on the table staring at him. "You look bored, Marshmallow." Tony scratched the cat's ears.

"Maybe it's because you don't understand what his day means!" He enthused and poured milk over his cereal. He also poured a small bowl of milk for Marshmallow.

Tony hummed as he made his way to the front room to turn on the morning news. Surely the police would have gotten his message and no doubt they'd delivered it to Al. Now, all he had to do was go pay a visit to Al under the guise of celebrating his possible success.

He plopped down in his recliner and took a bite of his cereal before setting it aside and picking up the two gift bags on the floor. If Al lost the election, he had a present prepared for him. It was a simple gift, a picture frame, so he could enjoy having his family around him. Tony pulled the picture frame out of the gift bag and scoffed, shaking his head. "Perfect."

The second gift bag contained the gift Al would receive if he won the election. Tony pulled the gun out of the bag and twisted the silencer on it. Six shots and everything would be over. No doubt after the threat from last night, Al would have his entire family at the office with him and Detective Krenshaw would be standing guard.

He'd take care of Detective Krenshaw first.

Bang!

Next would be the children.

Bang-Bang-Bang!

Mrs. Norton, the wicked witch herself. He'd hit her twice.

Bang-Bang!

Finally, he would be face to face with a torn, lost Dan Norton who would be on his knees begging to be spared. Tony laughed. "Oh, it's almost too perfect!"

He set the bags aside and skipped back to his bedroom to get dressed. This would be a day for the history books! People would forever remember his name in fear and Dan Norton's name in disgrace.

*****

"This is absurd! You can't keep us locked up in here like criminals!" Renee Norton put her hands on her hips, once more attempting to persuade Allie to let her go have lunch with her friends.

"Mrs. Norton, I've told you before, you cannot leave this room. It's for your own protection.

Someone is after your husband and if they are after him, they are after you as well. Your lives have been threatened and I have been assigned to guard you."

"So why can't you guard me at The Plaza?"

"Oh Renee, shut up and let the woman do her job!" Dan groaned and rubbed his face with his hands.

"Shut up? You're the one that comes from a psycho family. For all we know, it's your brother or sister doing all of this."

Allie winced and sank down in a chair in the corner. She hated seeing parents fight. Some of the worst fights she'd seen had been couples fighting. Allie glanced over at the three children sitting on the floor in the corner. It was too bad she couldn't get them out of the room.

"You jealous witch! Keep my family out of this! There is nothing wrong with my family."

"Oh please, Dan." Renee motioned to the room around them. "All of this, you got it because of me. Your family has been tearing you down but it's been me that has been behind you lifting you back up."

"My *family* has been tearing me down? It isn't my family that criticizes everything I do! As I recall, that's my *wife*!"

"Right. And I suppose it's also my fault that you slept with that slut in your campaign and got her pregnant!"

"Don't you talk about her like that." Al pointed his finger mere inches from his wife's face. "Jenna and I were in love, something I doubt your heart of stone could ever feel."

Allie's head snapped up and she hurried to stop the argument. "Jenna? Are you talking about Jenna Cortland?"

"See? Even she knows your *slut*." Renee looked at Allie. "Can you believe he got her pregnant, paid her to keep her quiet and then paid even more to get that child sent somewhere to be adopted?" Renee scoffed. "He spent a small fortune on that girl when he should have just gotten rid of that illegitimate scandal."

Dan's teeth clenched. "That's my son you're talking about."

Allie squeezed her eyes shut. "Hold on. Are you telling me that you slept with Jenna Cortland and had a child with her?" Renee opened her mouth to answer, but Allie held up her hand and stopped her. "No one is talking to you. Mr. Mayor, is it true?"

Dan sighed and nodded. "It's true."

"How did you meet her?"

"She was on Kent Bradley's campaign team. We met at one of the social events and hit it off. We were only together one night. When she came back to tell me about the baby, she talked to my secretary who told Renee about it. They made the decision to force this girl to abort my son." Dan glared at his wife. "That wasn't at all what I wanted. I abhor abortion."

"Go on."

Dan sighed. "Well, when I found out, I went to see Jenna myself. We talked and made the decision to put the child up for adoption. We stayed together for several months. When her pregnancy started to show and we couldn't hide it anymore, we had to part ways until after the baby was born. However, Renee threatened to divorce me if I saw her again and I knew if that happened my political career would be over before it even started."

Allie nodded, starting to put the final pieces together in her mind. "How many people knew about your affair with Jenna Cortland?"

Dan looked at his wife. "Did you tell anyone?"

Renee scoffed. "You're joking. Like I'd actually admit that to someone."

Dan looked at Allie. "My secretary knew, my brother, Jenna didn't have any family, but I'm sure she told her friend Haylee Jameson. Those girls were really close, like sisters."

Allie pulled out her phone and called Megan. The phone rang several times before going to voicemail. "Megan, I need you to find any and all close associates of Haylee Jameson, Jenna's friend. Call me back as soon as possible with whatever you find."

Dan sighed and shook his head. "What does Jenna have to do with anything?"

"Whoever killed Jenna knew about the relationship you'd had with her. Haylee could have told anyone if she knew you were the father. That's leverage. It also explains what your campaign files were doing under Jenna's bed."

"It does?"

"She thought you wanted to abort her baby and that was going to be her revenge. You showing up stopped that. The killer didn't know about the bad blood." Allie stopped and shook her head. "The killer didn't know about the bad blood, so it couldn't have been Haylee. Unless Haylee told someone about the affair but not about the fight."

"Are you telling me whoever is killing all these people they're doing it because of what I did with Jenna? Why would they kill Jenna if they were avenging a wrong done to her?"

"They don't care about Jenna, but they know that you cared for her. This person is out to destroy you, to destroy everything you stand for." Allie narrowed in on Dan. "Do you know anyone who would want to exact this kind of revenge on you? Any enemies who would seek to destroy everything you're building?"

Before he could answer a knock sounded on the door. Allie asked if they were expecting company. They weren't. Allie pulled her gun out, flipping off the safety. Taking a deep breath she opened the door a crack. A man stood in the doorway with two gift bags. "This floor is blocked. Can I help you?"

"I'm Dan's brother. They told me I could come up."

Allie studied his brown eyes and easy-going smile. The man looked a lot like Dan. They had to be brothers. Allie opened the door to let him in. "Come on in." Allie put her gun away as she closed the door.

"Tony!" Dan exclaimed. "What are you doing here?"

"I'm here to support you. Win or lose."

*****

Marcus felt his phone vibrating and pulled it out. He didn't recognize the number, but answered it anyway. "Marcus."

"Long time no see."

His back stiffened, his grip on the phone tightened. "Nate, you better have a good reason for calling."

"I do, but you're going to have to trust me."

"Ha! Right, because trusting you is always best." Marcus glanced around him for any sign of the lying psychopath he was on the phone with. "Why don't you come talk to me face to face like a real man?"

"I would, but there's not time for that. Allie's in trouble."

Marcus frowned. "What do you mean? She's part of a protection detail right now."

"Yeah, some protection detail. They let the killer walk right into the building and Allie just let him in the room with them. I hope you're close by. If I go in there and save her life that kiss you gave her will mean nothing."

"What?" Marcus exclaimed. "How can you even know about that?"

Nate laughed. "You'd be amazed at what I know. Now get off the phone and go save the girl. Don't be too surprised when you see the target."

The call ended and Marcus sighed, running for his car. Why had he left the mayor's office? He should have sent someone else to get dinner for the happy family. One thing he knew for sure, he was getting tired of Nate Harris. It was past time for that man to be caught and put behind bars.

At the moment though, if Nate was right, Allie was in danger. He had no reason not to doubt. If Nate was wrong, he'd look like a fool; but if Nate was right, he'd be a hero. It was a risk he was willing to take.

17

She'd seen her fair share of dysfunctional family relationships in her life, but the relationship between Dan and Tony Norton was by far the most dysfunctional. As soon as Tony had walked into the room, Dan had gone from concerned to angry and bitter. There was no brotherly love between the two. While Tony showed up acting as if he had Dan's best interest at heart, it was obvious he resented his brother.

Tony had been in the room ten minutes. She'd been ready for him to leave ten minutes ago. The polls would be in soon and the winner would be announced. Part of her was relieved it was about to be over, but what if it being over meant someone would lose their life?

Allie watched Tony from her chair in the corner. The man stood straight, his shoulders back. She'd seen that not too long ago. The entire time they had questioned Jonathan Bradley, he'd sat straight up in his chair. Allie frowned and continued watching Tony. The way the man paced was in slow, even steps.

He was wearing boots, very similar to the boots she saw at the Kentlee's house. Allie swallowed hard and took a calming breath. If she made the wrong move now, there were five people who could get caught in the cross fire. She had to be sure.

Allie jumped when her phone vibrated against her backside. Sighing, she reached for the phone, keeping her eyes on Tony. "Krenshaw."

"Allie, it's Megan. I did some searching on Haylee. She was friends with Jenna for several years. She'd had her fair share of boyfriends and one of them stuck out to me. She dated a man named Anthony Norton. Because of the last name, I checked and he's Mayor Norton's older brother. He was shipped off to military school when he was thirteen. As far as I can tell, he's been living in his younger brother's shadow for years."

"Good job." Allie swallowed hard. She had to choose her next words very carefully. She stared down at the carpet, feeling Tony's eyes on her.

"Do you want me to track down his location?" Megan asked.

"No need."

"No need? What do you mean? This is our guy! It has to be! He has a military record, a pretty good connection with one of the victims, *and* he is related to the mayor with reason to be mad. I really think we should find this guy."

"No, Megan. There's no need." Why couldn't the girl take a hint?

Megan gasped. "Oh my, do you know where he is?"

"Yes, like I said." Allie saw Tony move toward the gift bags. There had to be a gun in one of the bags, but which one?

"A team is on the way now. I'll give Marcus a call."

"All right, keep up the good work. We'll find him." Allie hung up and slipped her phone into her pocket with a sigh.

"No luck?" Dan asked.

Allie shook her head. "Nothing."

"There has to be some kind of clue, some easy way of finding this guy!" Dan ran his hand through his hair. "I thought you and Marcus were the best. I guess I was wrong."

Allie saw her chance and took it. She stood up and confronted Dan. "Excuse you, Marcus and I have the best closure rate in the city. You should be thankful we're still here. We could be anywhere, but we chose to stay here in this dump with lousy pay."

"Really? Someone is out there trying to kill me. You can't seem to find him and you choose *now* to bring up your pay? Maybe your pay is just a reflection of the work you do."

"How dare you! I've given up two years of my life for this!" Allie saw Tony step back and lean against the wall, seeming to enjoy the show.

"Maybe if you were better at your job and gave us better supplies and facilities, I could perform my job better."

"Supplies and facilities aren't everything. A bit of common sense is needed too. Apparently you're lacking in that department."

"Common sense really isn't that common." Renee chimed in.

"You stay out of this." Allie snapped and narrowed her eyes at Dan. "You know what, if you don't think I'm competent enough to do this job, maybe I should just leave."

"Well maybe you should! Locking my family in a room is something I could have done without your help!" Dan shook his head and pointed at the door. "Get out of here!"

"I won't leave until my captain dismisses me."

"Ha!" Dan walked over to the phone and pushed one of the speed dials. "That can be arranged."

Allie worked her jaw, feeling humbled by everything that had been said to her. It was all said in anger and not true, but the verbal beating she got from Dan was one she gave herself almost every day. Allie glanced at the clock on the wall. Ten minutes until the polls were in.

She watched Tony in her peripheral. He'd moved back over to the two gift bags. He stood closer to one than the other. The one closest to him would be the one with the gun. Was she faster than he was? What if he made it to the gun before she could stop him? She needed backup and backup was about ten minutes away.

*****

Even with the sirens blaring and lights flashing, it was still a fight to get through the downtown area. Marcus saw traffic ahead had come to a complete stop. "You've got to be kidding me." He craned his neck to see what was going on ahead. He spotted a minor car accident ahead. If he had more time he would walk up there and give the people a piece of his mind before demanding they move the non-injury accident from the middle of the street.

Time was of the essence.

Marcus grabbed his phone and slipped it in his pocket. He was four blocks from the mayor's office. He could make it. He took off running down the street, dodging the nosy bystanders taking pictures and video of the accident. He would never understand why people had to share everything that they saw in their lives.

He spotted a frog in the gutter. "Oh look, a frog, I should stop and put that online somewhere. It could be my new profile picture." He mocked and dodged one final bystander. With his path cleared, he took off at a dead run to get to Allie. Their first kiss would *not* be their last.

*****

The mayor was getting impatient on the phone. Finally, he gave up and replaced the handset on the receiver. "Where is your captain?"

"Well, the election's today and one of the candidates have been threatened. If I were a guessing person, I'd say he was out taking care of that at the moment." Allie shrugged. "But that's just me using common sense."

Dan narrowed his eyes at her and came around the desk.

At the same, Renee turned on the TV. "It's time! The polls are in!" Renee grabbed her husband's arm. "When you're re-elected, you can have her fired. Let's see what the numbers are."

Everyone's attention was on the TV, including Tony. Allie continued to watch him. She casually rested her hand on her gun, checking to make sure the safety was off and it was ready to fire. She had one target, but there were five other people Tony could target.

The polls were up.

Allie glanced at Dan and Renee. Their hands were clenched tight together; both excited to see the results of the election. Tony had reached into the gift bag. She could almost envision his sausage fingers wrapped around the 9mm he'd shot Bobbi with.

Renee's squeal bounced off the walls.

Dan Norton had just been re-elected.

Allie pulled out her gun and aimed it at Tony's head. Tony pulled out his gun, aiming it at Allie. "Don't do this Tony. Put that gun down."

Dan, realizing what was happening stepped forward to confront his brother. Tony had a new target.

"Not another move, Dan! I swear I'll do it!"

"In front of the kids? Come on, Tony, this isn't you. Why are you doing this?"

"Why?" Tony scoffed, his teeth clenched. "Do you have *any* idea what it's like to live in the shadow of the great Dan Norton?" He shook his head. "Not only that, but also your *little* brother. I'm supposed to be proud, I guess, but I hate you. I've always hated you."

"Tony, you need to put that gun down. It's not going to solve anything." Allie inched her way between Dan and Tony's gun. Dan was taller than she was and she had no doubt Tony could take the head shot. She just wasn't sure he would. "We can discuss all of this downtown."

"All those people, Tony? You killed those people. *Children!*"

"Dan, I've got this." Allie mumbled over her shoulder.

"No, I didn't kill those people, you did. *You* killed them when you rejected me time and again. *You* killed them when you refused to let me come to the family dinner on Sunday. You're ashamed of me, you hate me and I don't understand why."

"Tony, you're sick. You need help. Let me help you, okay? Maybe we can have a family dinner."

"This isn't about the dinner!" Tony yelled. He took a few steps forward, his gun leveled at Dan's head.

"Tony, you lower that gun or I'll shoot you where you stand."

Tony met her eyes. She knew that look. He was ready to die. He'd come here today prepared to leave in a body bag. "Not until I've finished." Tony took a step back and aimed his gun at the children in the corner.

"Tony, don't do it!" She yelled.

The door opened behind her and Marcus appeared next to the children, his gun aimed at Tony's head. "I'd do as the lady says, Tony."

He looked beyond Marcus to the children. "Say your final good night to Mommy and Daddy." He said in a sing song voice.

The children cried and hugged each other close.

Allie wasn't sure who fired first but two gunshots echoed in the room.

*****

"I was beginning to wonder if you were going to show up."

Marcus sighed and shook his head. "I should have known my heroic entrance would be unappreciated." Marcus joined her in leaning against the squad car. "That was a nice shot."

"You too." Allie glanced at him out of the corner of her eye. "Question, what is your real first name? We both know your name isn't Handsome Marcus."

Marcus looked at her in mock surprise. "You really think I would go through so much trouble for Bastian's benefit? I don't think so." Marcus shook his head. "I can't believe you don't believe me."

"Ha!" Allie shook her head. "Sorry, I really don't. I will get to the truth, though."

Marcus smiled and crossed his arms over his chest. "Do you want to give me a ride to the car pound?"

Allie frowned. "The car pound?"

"Yeah, I left my car sitting in traffic. There was an accident and I had to get here, so I just left it." Marcus grinned. "See? Totally heroic. That's something you'd see in the movies. The hero running four blocks to save the heroine in a blaze of bullets!"

    Allie laughed. "Right, that's so true." Allie bit her lip and glanced up at him. "There is one thing missing from this movie."

    Marcus pushed away from the car and turned to face her. "Hero makes it in time to save the heroine. Bad guy has two bullets in his head. Hostages are all alive and well. What's missing?"

    "If you have to ask…"

    He smiled and grabbed her hand, pulling her close. "Oh, I don't have to ask."

    "I'm glad you finally got the courage to kiss me."

Marcus scoffed. "Are you kidding? Maybe if I'd had a little encouragement over the years, I could have acted on it!"

Allie laughed and wrapped her arms around his neck. "Shut up and kiss me, Handsome."

About Rae

Rae Burton is an award winning mystery author from the Midwest. She enjoys writing mystery and suspense novels, as well as some historical romances. Currently she is working on the third installment of The Krenshaw Files.

Coming March 2016:

"A blackmailed killer is still a killer."
-Detective Marcus

The time has come for a notorious hit man to be stopped. Will Detective Krenshaw be able to look past her feelings for him to put an end to his killing?

Made in the USA
San Bernardino, CA
21 November 2015